$\mathcal{B}$ as in $\mathcal{B}$eirut

B as in Beirut

by Iman Humaydan Younes
translated by Max Weiss

Interlink Books

An imprint of Interlink Publishing Group, Inc.
Northampton, Massachusetts

First published in 2008 by

INTERLINK BOOKS
An imprint of Interlink Publishing Group, Inc.
46 Crosby Street, Northampton, MA 01060
www.interlinkbooks.com

Library of Congress Cataloging-in-Publication Data
Yunus, Iman Humaydan.
[Ba' mithla bayt—mithla Bayrut. English]
B as in Beirut / by Iman Humaydan Younes ; translated by
Max Weiss.
p. cm.
ISBN 978-1-56656-709-1 (pbk.)
I. Weiss, Max, II. Title.
PJ7874.U475B313 2007
892.7'36—dc22
2007026206

Printed and bound in the United States of America

To request our complete 40-page full-color catalog,
please call us toll free at 1-800-238-LINK, visit our
website at www.interlinkbooks.com, or write to
Interlink Publishing
46 Crosby Street, Northampton, MA 01060
e-mail: info@interlinkbooks.com

Contents

ℒilian

*T*here was nothing of mine left in the closet. Everything I would need had been packed into suitcases. Lama and Karim hadn't been to school since last term. I tried teaching them myself for one, two days before I gave up. I packed my clothes into suitcases a month ago, leaving out a pair of jeans and some sports clothes. When Talal saw me opening the suitcases repeatedly to re-pack them, he asked me where I was going. Every time he asked this question, I gave him the same answer: I'm going to my brother Tony's in Australia. I'll find work there. I'll work with him in the restaurant, washing dishes or cooking, or I'll teach music. A chasm of silence separated Talal's query from my response. I would avoid answering other questions that followed. While I waited, I'd distract myself from the conversation going on all around me by reading novels that Josefa left me, novels about characters who led lives that didn't resemble ours one bit.

All of my clothes and all of the kids' were in suitcases. Whenever I needed something, I would have to dump the suitcase out to find it. I tried to organize everything in different suitcases, putting my clothes in one and the kids' stuff in another. I repeatedly emptied the contents onto the rug. I shook the dust off and re-packed everything. I set the kids' clothes aside. Then I would begin to re-fold every piece of clothing: Cotton shirts on one side, pants on the other. I rolled up the underwear and tucked it into the corners of the suitcase. After that, I stared at the open-jawed suitcases and moved in to close them, secretly rejoicing at the triumph of my skill and precision. Clothes—clean, organized, ironed and folded—just waiting to move from one place to another with me. After a while, the whole thing started to seem absurd. I went back to mixing the clothes in with all the other stuff. I threw it all into the suitcases helter skelter. I said that this didn't tire me out, but maybe even gave me strength. I would wake up in the morning and my eyes would dart straight to the suitcases to make certain they were still in the same place, closed and waiting. I mused how they were just like me in that way: closed and waiting. I waited just to cross the doorstep, consumed by a passion that I couldn't keep to myself. I waited for my travel documents and visa. I counted days endlessly . When we submitted our immigration application to the embassy in Cyprus, Talal had been excited to emigrate. He said that it would make him feel better and he would have more time to devote exclusively to writing. He traveled with us to Cyprus the first time and when they told us at the embassy that we were going to have to wait, we came back here to wait even more.

When we scurried to the bomb shelter, I would carry whatever suitcases I could with me. Talal used to get upset with my fussiness, the amount of stuff in my arms. I had no choice, I told myself sometimes: what if we had to stay in the shelter for several days? Didn't I have to be prepared, to take food with me, or blankets, games, and books? Once I had arranged everything to take to the shelter, I would stand up and take stock again, to make sure I had everything I needed. I also thought: what if a rocket were to crash into our house, sending the walls and curtains flying, scattering everything from our closets, leaving everything only as scraps on the floor. I kept our passports with me in the small straw purse that was slung over my shoulder wherever I went. The thought of losing them terrified me.

Talal moved closer to pick up some bags, muttering some words of protest about my fussiness and the amount of stuff. "Do you really need all of this?" he asked, in what sounded like derision, nodding his head toward the pile of plastic bags and small suitcases on the ground all around me. He bent over and tried to open the bags so he could see what was inside and leave behind in the apartment whatever he thought unnecessary. But I shoved his hand aside, unaffected by his comments, and re-sealed the bags. About to lose my patience with him, I said, "Go downstairs, go on down. I don't want your help. Just take Lama with you." Whenever she saw what was happening, Maha would help me, and even though he never went into the shelter with us, Ghassan helped me, too, picking my stuff up and walking downstairs behind me. He set our things outside the shelter door and went back up to Maha's apartment.

I didn't see Maha as much after Ghassan died. I continued visiting her regularly during the first few months following his death. Sometimes she would go to her hometown in the mountains and stay there for weeks at a time. When she came back, she would tell me how resolved she'd become: to change her lifestyle, to paint her apartment a different color, reupholster the chairs, change the curtains. Then, as time went by and the war dragged on, Maha went back to sleeping in Warda's apartment or in the bomb shelter, having changed nothing. She started having panic attacks, as though she were on the verge of suffocating. Whenever I was with her and this happened, she told me to squeeze her wrist. "Squeeze here! Here!" She pulled me toward her interlocked hands and nodded toward her wrists, as though she would have grasped them herself if she had a third hand. "Please, I feel like I can't breathe!" Then I stopped hearing her voice as she was talking to me, hearing only the groans of air, warm from her chest. She worked her mouth like someone who had lost the power of speech.

Before Ghassan's death, our nights had been glorious. I felt sometimes as though we'd been friends since the beginning of time, not since college. During our evenings together, Ghassan used to serenade us. I was struck by Maha's unusual ability to wait. She was a few years older than Ghassan yet she went on waiting for the day she would be able to marry him. Whenever I asked her what they were waiting for, she said that Ghassan's mother hadn't agreed yet, adding, "She'll agree someday, I know she will."

Our late nights together stopped when Ghassan died. I remember how Talal used to tell me about the stories he was writing for publication. It had been a long time since he'd finished one. He hadn't completed anything at all for some years. He had a pile of story beginnings:

amputated stories with unknown endings. For a long time, he used to say, "I'm going to write a novel." That was during college. When I asked him later if he remembered saying that, he always said no. Had his memory been transformed into pain? Did my questions hurt him, too? I saw how he would press his hand against his stomach and say, "Aaakh." He never wanted to talk. Conver-sation disappeared, and in its disappearance, I could read all the small things scattered by silence and waiting.

I was still pregnant with Karim when Talal's family fled from the South to live with us. The already small house grew even smaller. Our customs changed, Talal's and mine. We had to come up with new arrangements that would be suitable for a space that was growing more cramped by the day. I started waiting in antici-pation for the evening to arrive. Alone in our room, my body clung to his. I'd slide my hand along his smooth skin as if getting to know him all over again. I'd watch him edit what he'd written. I'd scrunch my face up in the folds of his neck and chest, trace his outline with my lips and nose and smell his scent, close my eyes and breathe it in deep for a long time. I'd hold my breath as though I could hide these odors in my soul. He set his papers aside and drew me to him, smiling as he wrapped his arms around me and said, "You're on very dangerous ground..."

Many things happened. Little things piled up and strung our lives together. We might remember them all, or we might just remember some of them, but we certainly won't ever understand their trajectories. At some point we must accept our affairs as they are; questions become luxuries. Our life becomes the continuous disappointment of our childhood dreams and a pain that grows deeper every morning. We suffer when we are born, when we love, when we leave, when we are left behind, until there is nothing to do but to laugh in the face of our pain.

Talal's family spread themselves throughout the house. They moved around freely and put their things away wherever they pleased. Talal's mother and father slept in the little room with Lama. Talal's sister Salwa and his brother Abbas, who was getting ready to travel to Germany, slept in the corner of the salon that the dinner table had occupied; Talal had taken it apart and placed it near the wall in the living room before his family had arrived. We started eating on a low table or sometimes in the kitchen. We stopped making plans. I fought my irritation with a pragmatism that sapped all of my strength, as though I were convincing myself I was a practical woman and that in days of violence such as these it didn't befit a practical woman to live freely in her own home or to be intimate with her husband, whom she no longer saw except with other people around.

My desire to leave the country once and for all had increased ever since the accident in which Talal lost his right hand. "I want to get out of here," I used to repeat whenever Talal was present-yet-absent and whenever there were empty wine bottles at his side. "We're already gone, we don't have to go anywhere," the words slid out of his mouth, heavy and slow: "Let's go while we're still here," he mocked me. "People emigrate so they can come home with money. Why are we emigrating? To come back with lost time? Revolution and love are a lot like life: you can't ever repeat them, so don't bother trying." He fell silent for a moment and then turned up his head to look at me, except he didn't look at me. He shut his eyes again and leaned his head back. "D'you think anything will change if you go?" I said I wanted to go for Lama and Karim's sake. "Run away then, hide behind your children!" Was I running away from Talal, from the terror enveloping the city, or from the silence that conversation couldn't seem to break? Was I running away from myself, who no longer had a safe haven, from where I was born, or from the alienation of this place?

Talal turned on the radio. The broadcaster's voice buzzed with a new story. I went over and turned the volume down. He yelled. I didn't respond. He walked over and turned it up. I turned it down. He turned it up even louder. I turned it off.

Ever since the accident, Talal had stopped going to the newspaper. He sat at his desk with a pen in his hand, wrote one word, put the pen down. Asked his mother, the hajjeh, for a cup of coffee. Got a bottle of wine. Poured a glass. Returned to the desk. Picked up the pen. Wrote. The coffee arrived. Got cold. He erased what he'd written. He picked up the piece of paper, crumpled it into a ball with one hand and threw it onto the ground, like all the pieces before it. He filled the circular copper ashtray with cigarette butts. He drained the bottle of wine.

It was hard for him to write with his left hand after his right arm had been amputated. It was like learning how to write for the first time all over again. "I don't have anything to write anymore. What do you want me to write? Where's my hand? Is it still lying in the street where the ambulance driver picked me up, or did the surgeon cut it off?" He added, "My hand has a story that I don't know so I can't write about it." "What's the difference," I asked, "if your hand is still flopping around in the street, mixed with blood and water from the fire truck, or if it got thrown away in some hospital trashcan like something nobody wanted?"

Cold sweat accumulated on his brow as he lay in the hospital bed. The nurse dabbed at his face and neck with a paper towel then cast it aside, soaked. She wiped him down with another one.

His body started to convulse. It took some time
for him to calm down. After she injected the
painkiller, she left. I caressed his shoulder lightly.
I ran my fingers through his hair. I pulled my face
in close to him. The wrinkles on his face unfolded
for a few moments, then quickly tightened up
again. I kissed him. A hint of a smile passed
across his lips. I knew that he was distant then,
having spent the past six nights with nightmares
that took him somewhere I couldn't follow.
"Where's my hand?" he murmured, squeezing his
left fist into a ball. He stroked his wrist, the most
painful spot. The pain was still searing, in revolt
on the borders of his body, as it had when he was
first injured. He withdrew into silence. The room
was perfectly quiet. I crossed the short distance
between his bed and the broad window. Warning
sirens pierced the cement blocks and rang in my
ears. Distant explosions faded away quickly into
quiet. From the window, I could see the blue sea,
a vast ocean clinging to the sky, a wide sky
without limits. I imagined a woman standing on
the windowsill, flapping her arms in the wind like
a bird trying to fly for the first time. She rose into
the air, chased the sky without knowing where
she might end up.

I sat on the plastic covering the metal chair.
An artificial smell like the one you find in a five-
star hotel lingered in the air. I sat there for hours
waiting for one of his eyelashes to stir, for him to

open his eyes and ask for something. I saw his
head move. I jumped up. I stood up, drew closer
to him. I leaned my head over so my ear could
graze his lips. The warmth of his breath stung me.
Nothing.

It had been many nights since I last slept in
my own bed. I sent Lama and Karim to stay with
my sister Janet. She came to visit Talal and took
the two of them with her to Ajaltoun. I stopped
looking at the clock hanging in the waiting room
on the first floor, where Talal lay. I got used to a
time without numbers or hours. The attending
nurse threw her head down on the table in front
of her. Behind the thin glass, she was like a faded
portrait in a frame. I woke her to tell her that it
was time for his medicine. She gazed at me
through half-closed eyes. She nodded her head
slightly, as though she were used to hearing such
things. Then she threw herself back down on the
table, her arms beneath her head. When I roused
her a second time, she murmured something
without looking at me, as if talking to herself: the
gist was that I should thank God for finding my
husband an empty bed in the hospital at all; who
cares if she was a little late giving him his medicine.

The night was silent and gloomy. I heard
footsteps in the corridor. I shivered. I stood up
and walked on my bare feet. Dim lights slid along
the shiny white walls, illuminating the cold place
and making the loneliness seeping into my bones

worse. I waited for somebody to pass by, anybody—a patient, a doctor or a nurse, or someone, like me, who couldn't sleep. I wanted someone to pass by, someone I'd stop and ask to have a cigarette with me. We'd drink a cup of coffee that I'd pour from the pot Maha brought. I'd talk about Talal, about me, about Talal's hand and its absence. Perhaps I'd move closer to that person, whether it was a man or a woman, and ask him or her to wrap their warm arms around me. The person would tell me that what was happening wasn't real, that Talal was fine, that nothing had changed. The person would tell me that everything going on outside was an illusion, a game, no more than child's play. I waited for something to happen but nothing ever did. The room remained silent. The only thing that broke the silence was the creaking of a door slowly opening, then closing again. Outside, the air whistled softly. Through the windowpane, I saw the stubs of tree branches swaying high and lonely. When the wind nudged them toward the building, their rustling along the wall repeatedly interrupted the chilly silence, telling me that life continued outside.

There was a painful weight in my legs and my head ached. I stood up. I shut the door. I returned to the cold metal chair. I stretched out and covered myself with a thin gray blanket. Images of Lama and Karim flickered before my slowly closing eyes and I was overcome with a yearning to see them. Sleep finally took me despite the cold stiffness in my limbs.

I stopped going to the conservatory, even after Talal had been released from the hospital. There was a new life awaiting me. He protested at first when I accompanied him to the bathroom, undid the buttons of his shirt and helped him take off his underwear. He stood in the tub and I asked him to sit down on the chair I had placed there specifically for him. I lathered soap on the sponge and scrubbed his back. He jerked back from the touch of my hands. The hairs on his arms and shoulders stood up. He said he was cold, so I scrubbed the warm sponge against his body faster. I broke the unbearable silence to tell him about Karim and Lama. I told him stories that almost managed to fill the chasm growing between us. Talal remained silent. I knew that he couldn't stand uncertainty, but I also knew that the silence I was trying to break was all too real, for certain. I doused him with warm water. Then I wrapped my arms around him and kissed his somewhat stiff neck. "Enough, that's enough, get out of here! I can take care of myself." I wasn't sure he realized what he was saying. I didn't get out. Instead, I dried him off and helped him get dressed.

I'd wake up to the sound of Talal's voice and his seizures. I couldn't understand what he was saying. His voice was like that of someone choking: rasping and wailing. Like someone in the throes of an argument they can't end. He opened his eyes, looked at me. The muscles in his face relaxed. He closed his eyes and went back to sleep. I finally lost all sense of security when Talal's nightmares started. What if the life we'd had together never returned? What if the man sleeping in the bed before me was no longer the man I used to know? Maha was speaking to me. I couldn't hear what she was saying. I pretended to be listening. One thought and one thought alone cycled through my mind: we are all alone. We lose those who we love, alone, and there is no shelter outside of the womb.

I used to say I had no choice but to be with this man and push him onward. With a vague, instinctual fear, I made things up as I went along. I saw myself as a woman afraid of heights standing on the edge of a cliff; all it would take to fall was the slightest push. I saw the very thing I wanted to avoid growing inside me, surging forth like a raging river. I saw love and death in other things we did when we were at our loneliest. What is left for us after we discover that the life we lived wasn't a dream after all, but that what we had been waiting for was the dream? Yet waiting continued to fill our lives.

In the past, when desire first awakened in me, Talal used to come to me and penetrate me like rushing water after a drought. I used to quench my thirst even when it really hurt. Was it pain or limitless fear carrying me to new realms? I started napping whenever I felt like it. And from then on, whenever the violence of distant places drew near, I wasn't awoken by Karim's crying or the words he mumbled in this sleep: *Tar... taq... tartaq*, he repeated. I wasn't awoken by the words Lama blurted out while she was sleeping either: words from various languages that came out garbled and incomprehensible.

When he used to come to me, I'd experience something like flying: high above the earth like colored birds that rise and sing with mesmerizing lightness. From there, I could see that dreams do come true sometimes, even the most far-fetched. I'd dream at the strangest moments. "Do dreams have a smell?" I asked him. He responded: "It's scary, when dreams become possible, become reality, become truth." Dreams are scary indeed, but what of the truth? What is the truth that we were living, that I bore witness to, that he witnessed, or that Abbas witnessed?

I don't know why I'm thinking about all of this right now. I daydream about how my facial muscles relaxed when Talal made love to me. My drawn skin loosened and became smooth to the touch. For a few moments, I could hear rain

droplets beating against the windows of our
room. Our room: our only sovereign territory as
long as his family occupied the rest of the house.
It was early autumn. An early rain. I buried my
face in his neck and smelled his pungent sweat.
A brief torrent of ecstasy came over me as the
smell of wet earth seeped in through the window
and blended with the scents of love coming from
the bed.

He pulled out of me abruptly the moment he'd
finished. I remained in bed, lit a cigarette and
smoked it deeply and slowly. He stood in front of
the open window and leaned his head down
toward the base of the building, toward the
shadowy street. His body was being pulled
outside. He started talking without even turning
to look at me. "Are you talking to me or to the
neighbors?" I asked him with mild reproach. I
caught a glimpse of a fleeting, cheerful smile on
his face even as he turned away from me. He
didn't move, just reached out his only hand
toward me. I handed him the cigarette I had just
lit. Sex still managed to smooth out the lines in
his face that had grown even more pronounced,
still stoked a fire in his eyes. I saw him as he had
always been, even at the moment he came. His
eyes lingered on my face for a few moments.
Then he went distant, as though he had no

connection with what his body was doing, as
though his body had its own private world that he
couldn't access, like someone who had misplaced
his keys. I no longer closed my eyes, but instead
started amusing myself the moment we united by
looking for any changes to appear on his face. I
focused on my womb as it opened into an
expanded emptiness, on my body, no longer
caring whether it belonged to me. But a problem
weighed on my mind. I saw how our bodies grew
accustomed to the alienation that had come
between us and slept in our bed once we had
fallen asleep. I saw how both of our bodies
accommodated those moments that were so
lonely for me, that were so lonely for Talal, when
he penetrated the deepest recesses of my being.

There were many things Talal had to get used to,
including an entirely different body, nothing like
his old one. He looked flustered when he was
unable to button his shirt all by himself. When
he extended his left hand to shake someone else's,
he acted as if it didn't bother him, as though these
were ordinary things that were happening, as
though nothing had changed. He stopped
writing. Was that because he had lost his will, or
because he had lost his hand, as he used to say?
He stopped coming down to the bomb shelter,
too. I started sending Lama and Karim down

with their grandmother while he and I passed the night in Warda's first-floor apartment. We drank coffee that Maha made for us. Warda busied herself on our behalf by showing us pictures of her daughter. She would look at the pictures of Sara and tell us every last thing about her, repeating the story of her birth. Once her familiar raving got going, she would remind us that Sara must have been kidnapped somewhere in Beirut.

The Warda I once knew was no more, except for the jet-black hair that spilled down and covered her back. It was only like that because she neglected to get it cut. Warda got up suddenly, set the photo album aside and said that she could hear Sara's voice coming from in front of the building. "She must be playing down there. The bombing is getting closer. I'll just go down and get her." She crossed the parlor toward the door. Josefa grabbed her and brought her back, promising to go call for Sara herself. "All right, all right," Warda said, and walked back to the couch, totally calm. Josefa opened the outer door, crept out to the stairwell and leaned the upper half of her body over the railing. She pretended to talk to someone downstairs. She came back and told Warda that her daughter was fine, that she was inside, playing near the elevator, and would be up in a few minutes.

On the day Warda wanted to dye her jet-black hair blonde, Maha and I weren't sure what to do. "That's the color I want," she told us, pointing at a woman's picture in a magazine she was holding. I tried to imagine Warda with blonde hair. Maha told her, "You're beautiful just the way you are." I tried to convince her that Sara wouldn't be able to recognize her if she dyed her hair. Warda wasn't having it. When she opened the door and started heading upstairs, I knew that she was going to knock on Josefa's door and tell her about her new plan. Josefa would welcome her and placate us in her ever-pleasant tone, "It's all right, it's all right, maybe it'll do her some good." Josefa shut us all up when she said that this might benefit Warda; maybe the change would be good for her. Then she went down, bought some dye and helped her bleach her hair. How strange Warda looked with that colored hair and how much more appropriate the things she said seemed to this new look.

When Warda got sick and was wracked by chronic seizures, Josefa took care of her. She treated her with herbs that she collected herself. She said, "This one's for nerves, this one's for stomachaches, and this one's for bronchitis." She collected herbs to cure every illness. When Warda refused to get out of bed, claiming that her legs were paralyzed, Josefa carried her to the bathroom and sat her down on the small chair in the tub as though she were a little girl. That's when Warda told her all about her daughter, stories Josefa had already heard several times before. "That's true, you're right," Josefa repeated. She dried Warda off with a large towel and asked her what she wanted to wear. Warda always chose her old lace and silk dresses, which were bright like spring flowers: clothes she bought when her body was still like the bodies of other women. Wearing them now, she looked like an out-of-work clown. Her body was withered and shrunken. Had Josefa pushed any harder as she pressed her hand against Warda's bony shoulder to coax her into sitting, she might have crushed her brittle bones.

Josefa's home was different from anywhere we'd ever lived. Whenever she opened the door for me, everything about it enticed me to enter. Her influence was apparent on everything, in every corner. In the kitchen, small linen bags hung near the window that overlooked a balcony with a partial view of neighboring buildings; Josefa had covered it with perforated white wooden planks, which the sunlight streamed through. She converted her balcony into a garden replete with green plants that climbed toward the ceiling. In the small linen bags, Josefa put many varieties of herbs that she'd collected from the various places she'd visited. Then she started growing certain plant varieties herself. She invited me to sit down on the shaded yet somehow sunny balcony. There was a circular table in the middle surrounded by straw chairs with cushions she had sewn herself out of vibrant fabric. "Relax, stretch out your legs," she told me when I sat down. Then she cooed at her colorful canary, which was used to leaving its cage through the small aperture that was always left open, flying around the house and then perching comfortably on her shoulder. At that very moment, Josefa broke out into song. While she sang, she pushed her mouth so close to the canary's small beak that she nearly kissed it. The canary chirped and fluttered its wings. She repeated her song while she made coffee and the bird continued pacing back and forth on her shoulder. She sang her favorite song, which was in Spanish, a song about a woman who lost her bird and sat down to cry over it. A man came along and offered her his handkerchief. The woman dried her tears and smiled. When she looked around for the man, he was gone.

Josefa's home resembled her completely, much like the novels she lent me and I got addicted to reading novels about beautiful people whose passion for life was as powerful as a storm, people who loved and people who suffered.

Sometimes I told myself that these novels were works of pure fiction with no connection to reality. But Josefa actually resembled the heroines, who transformed their misfortunes into fertile wheat fields. She resembled these heroines when the wrinkles in her face bunched together. Her hands were always generous, leaving warm fingerprints on everything she touched. She looked so funny as she told me about her three ex-husbands. When Maha asked her which was closest to her heart, her eyes lit up with a glow that spread all over her face, and she replied, "My third husband Roberto, the Italian. When he saw me for the first time, he called me 'Auntie,' out of respect. Your aunt my ass, I told him. We got married in Venezuela. His strange behavior used to drive me crazy but I was also in love with his madness. Whenever he came by the house, I locked the bedroom door on purpose. My soul thrilled and I trembled when his footsteps beckoned me from the living room. I would answer from the bedroom, burning up at the thought of touching his body. He tried to open the door. He couldn't. He ordered me to open up. I told him no, that he should go away, that I didn't want to see him, even though I was actually dying to see him. He jiggled the doorknob several times, making a loud noise. I knew that he had begun to lose his mind. 'I told you to open up!' I told him that I would never open up for him. 'I don't want you right now, go on and tear the door off if you can.' His love for me struck like lightning when we were together. And when I got pregnant with Angelo, I could hardly believe it. I imagined it was a wicked tumor. Was it even possible for me to get pregnant at forty? If there was going to be rain, I should have clouded over much earlier, with one of my two ex-husbands. Maybe I got pregnant because I was in love with Roberto and because God wanted me to remember him forever. I gave birth to my only son and my son became my entire world. I was no longer interested in that man. I had a new man who I didn't fear would leave me one day if I got old. I didn't have to make myself beautiful every day or make myself smell nice just to turn him on. I started to ignore Roberto and to let him go out every night. He went on to break my heart with his constant nervousness. He slept in a different place every night. As though I was his mother and he had lost her. He came to me one day, piss drunk, and told me that he wanted to go off to search for diamonds in the Amazon with someone he'd met. I said, why not? Maybe I had secretly always wanted him to go travel, not because I didn't love him, but because my love for Angelo didn't leave room for me to be concerned about anyone else. At first, I got news about him. After a few years, I stopped hearing anything. Before returning to Lebanon with my son, I learned that he was living among an Amazonian tribe and that he had married one of their women."

Josefa told me all about her life and I used to be amazed by her stories. I wondered if it was really the story of her life she was telling me or the life of one of the characters in the novels she used to read.

I always wanted to stay at Josefa's for hours, to pretend her place was mine. But I was often prevented from going up to visit her because her apartment was on the top floor. She wasn't afraid, though. She wasn't afraid a day in her life. Sometimes she would stand out on the kitchen balcony at night, watching the explosions over the shrouded city light up the night sky. When she woke up the next day, she would say she wanted to cross over to the other side of the city to check on friends she hadn't heard from for a long time. She always mentioned her friends but rarely talked about her relatives, except for her son, who had recently moved to New York with a friend. It was as if she had no roots, as if she were a robust tree sprouting from nowhere. When she came back, she knocked on my door, gave me a handful of novels, and said, "Take these and read them. They're for you, I found

them in my son's library. He doesn't need them
anymore. He left his small place in Ashrafiyeh
and emigrated. Why should I leave them there?
Should I leave them there for the neighborhood
fighters who want to take over his apartment and
make it into a military headquarters? They said
the place was located in a military zone along the
front lines. I said they'd have to take it over my
dead body. One of them assaulted me, telling me
to go back where I came from, where my home
was: 'Nobody will bother you over there.' That
dog waited for me to tell him all about what was
happening to me here just so he could gloat over
it. All I told him was that Muslims were better
than the whole lot of them. I told him it was my
son's place back there and that I would never give
it up. Another fighter I knew well, and whose
mother I knew well, intervened, saying that
Angelo was a homosexual and a coward because
he refused to kill people. That dog would have
been dead if it weren't for me. I wish I'd left him
to die so that I wouldn't have had to hear such
vile things coming out of his mouth. When he
was born, he was stuck diagonally inside his
mother's birth canal. He would have asphyxiated
if I hadn't thrust my entire hand into that poor
woman's womb and pulled him out. At the
moment of his birth, he looked like a soggy blue
scrap of paper. And now look at him. He
squealed in my face like a wild pig."

I don't know what Josefa told them when she left her home on our side for the last time and moved to Ashrafiyeh. She said she didn't want to tell anyone anything. She didn't understand why the neighborhood fighters attacked her apartment, why they attacked the building where we lived, more than once. They came up to the fourth floor early one morning, knocked on her door and woke her up. When she opened the door, one of them smashed the door against the wall with his fist and she recoiled, staggering backward. He barged in and others followed, under the pretense that they needed to look through their binoculars at the view of East Beirut from her balcony. They spread out through the rooms of the house, opening closets, upending tables, taking things out of drawers and throwing them around. One of them asked her brusquely if there was someone staying with her and where he had gone, adding in a slow, icy voice, as though he were uncovering a crime: "What did you do in East Beirut yesterday?" "They're always messing with me, those sons of bitches. They're all the same, over here and over there: black dogs and white dogs." She said she wasn't angry, just sad, that she no longer felt comfortable, but afraid. "I understand they don't want me around, but over there, too! Where can I go without leaving the country? Lilian, my heart is broken."

Josefa never came back to our neighborhood. She passed through the checkpoint to visit her friends in East Beirut one last time and stayed there. I got a handful of novels from her and a few phone calls until news of her stopped entirely.

The children I used to give piano lessons to stopped coming to visit me. I had become accustomed to going to their homes until some of them quit practicing and left the country, while the rest simply stopped preparing for their lessons. I received a few letters from them: from Canada, Australia, and Cyprus. I had to find other work. Talal's brother Abbas started visiting us regularly. He had recently returned from Germany and was busy with his young wife and his activities with the Party members. I was surprised when he knocked on the door early one morning. After the accident he was never away for very long. He insisted that we go to the South or move somewhere else. "It's tucked away from everything going on here. As soon as the war heats up, it calms right down again. But here, there's no end to the war," he said, trying to convince us to go with him. There was an unspoken tension between Abbas and Talal. Talal wouldn't accept the idea of Abbas taking over Josefa's apartment in our building, Josefa who had moved to the other side of town. Talal said that

Abbas was embarrassing him. He asked Abbas why he held onto the apartment key even though he spent most of his time in either the southern suburbs or his hometown in the South. Abbas pretended he hadn't heard a word and started stroking his beard, which was thick and black and interwoven with short white whiskers.

Josefa left, but her voice still echoed in my memory. I left my apartment and went to Maha's. We hurried downstairs to Warda's. The fighters' voices echoed in the street. Idle chatter rose and seeped into our apartment building. Ranger's screeching voice boomed out whenever he called for Yusuf, the shopkeeper, to bring him more bottles of beer. I went home. Talal was quiet. The building was empty except for a few men and women, a few solitary women. I searched for a man. But I realized all men fall somewhere between Talal and Ranger.

A plastic tree stood in the corner of the living room this year. We called it a Christmas tree. Not much had changed outside. The streets were still dark. The headlights of the cars that passed sporadically in the void of the street provided a flicker of comfort before they darted away to seek shelter. Dim, tentative lights leaked through our windows, casting shadows in the gray rooms, lightening their melancholy, and exposing the loneliness of their inhabitants. The buildings were soundless. I didn't hear any children's voices or the footfalls of people rushing home. Holiday hordes appeared in front of me. I saw myself as a young child being hurried forward by my mother. She grabbed my hand and pulled me forward to keep up with her. My steps were rushed. She made certain I kept up with her. My hand wriggled away. I slowed down again. Things zoomed by as she pulled me along, colors I could no longer make sense of. I slowed down even more. I stopped altogether. The lights shining in the markets turned night into day. My mother stopped again. She swung around toward me, frantic, and motioned for me to hurry. We arrived at home. Everyone had been waiting for my mother. She unloaded all of her bags. The sound of clothes and toys being unwrapped rustled in my visceral memory. Tony and Janet were busy signing cards, including the card from me. "You're still too young," the two of them told me. "We can make more presents by writing cards," said Janet. In the large forest just outside of town, there were wild trees. My father selected a large specimen. "We found our Christmas tree," he said, and his tall frame disappeared into the house.

The history and timing of holidays has always intrigued me. I used to anticipate them like a little girl. I prepared myself for them and loved them. I relished the time we would spend making Oriental sweets during Ramadan, fresh-squeezed juice and fruit salad with nuts. There was a certain kind of folklore in the work that I adored. But I gave all of that up when Talal's family came to stay with us. During Ramadan, I had to avoid eating whenever his parents were around, and to yield the space in the kitchen to the hajjeh so she could prepare the foods she was accustomed to eating during that month back home: foods I didn't care for very much. I started slinking off during the hour she spent cooking for the breaking of the fast. I strapped Karim into his stroller and granted Lama the pleasure of pushing him around outside. On other occasions, I loaded both of them into the car and headed down to the seafront café. Once, I arrived to find the café totally empty of people. I sat down and ordered a bottle of beer from the waiter, who responded to my request with mild hesitation. "Beer!" he repeated. "You want beer?" he asked me dryly. I nodded without making eye contact with him. Why did he glare at me like that? Why did he feel the need to ask me twice? My voice was as clear as the sun that pierced my chilly bones. When he returned with my beer, I held it in my hands for a moment before deliberately handing it back to him. "I want it cold, ice cold," I told him, screwing my gaze on his face. He took back the bottle, re-screwed it and turned around, heading back to where he'd come from. I lit a cigarette and exhaled some smoke before letting out a deep sigh.

During the first few years of our marriage, Talal's brother Abbas would come up from the South with his parents. He would stay with us. I bought him new clothes for Christmas. We didn't have any children yet and I loved him as if he were my own son. But Abbas changed a lot that year. When he came in and saw the plastic tree, he commented curtly, "I don't care for this holiday. It's a sham. It's totally foreign to our history and identity, and Santa Claus is nothing but a big fat lie. I mean, he comes in a sleigh pulled by reindeer." Raising his arms, as though onstage addressing an audience, he added, "Reindeer, they say, reindeer! Do you see any fucking reindeer around here?!" I remember how Abbas used to help me chop a branch off a tree in the town forest for Christmas. My God, what a different person he was now that he was all grown up. He had become a different person altogether. He went to study in Germany and came back four years later with a young blonde woman on his arm. She seemed nervous when she appeared before the shaykh to sign the marriage certificate. When Abbas placed the scarf over her head, she looked like an overgrown little girl whose cheeks would turn scarlet whenever she got upset or laughed too hard. The scarf covered both sides of Andrea's rose-colored face and part of her broad forehead; her two blue eyes peered out from under it, conveying both curiosity and grief. Andrea told me, "I don't feel like going back to Germany. It's really boring there, but it's too scary to stay here. I don't know where to go." Whenever she came over, she would ask Talal to pour her a glass of wine. When she drank too much, she would start to cry, saying how she wished to return home to Germany and how she missed her mother. When Abbas became a figure in the Party, he took to locking Andrea in the house so she wouldn't be able to go out and buy booze. At that point, she started replacing wine with cheap liquor. She asked Talal for another glass and started eating voraciously. "All cities look alike," she used to say. "This place is a big prison and Germany is no different." Whenever Abbas came to Beirut, she hoped that he would bring her along. "I want to stay here with you," she told me when she came over. "I'm not afraid when I'm around you. Back in town, I'm afraid everywhere I go. Even in the bathroom, I'm afraid. Abbas won't talk to me very much anymore either. In the beginning, he would translate everything that visitors or friends said. Now, he won't even look at me. I thump him on the arm and ask what somebody just said. When everybody laughs, I want to know what they're laughing about so I can laugh with them. Abbas might glance at me and then go right on talking, without giving me an answer. I never hear my name anymore. The hajjeh calls me 'my daughter.' Abbas calls me 'Umm Mustafa,' and the neighbors call me 'Abbas's wife.' I wait for hours and hours just for the chance to call my family; when someone finally lifts the receiver and says hello, my heart soars. I speak with them, asking how they are and they ask how I am, and then I fall silent. I don't have anything more to say. I burst out crying at the sound of my mother's voice on the line, and she asks me what's wrong. I cry because her voice seems drowsy and uninterested. Abbas goes out at night. The guys always come over to pick him up. When they hang out late into the night over at one of their houses, I go with him to sit with the other women. They ask me about my boys Mustafa and Ahmad and then proceed to talk among themselves. When they start serving the plates of food, one of them swivels her head around toward Abbas and says, in a hushed English voice, as though she wants to be absolutely sure that I understand what she's about to say, 'Wild thyme is an aphrodisiac, you know.' Then she places the green leaves in her mouth and chews them, pressing her lips forward as though she wants to flip one of them over."

Andrea spoke to her two boys in German. The two boys spoke Arabic with everyone else. They only spoke German with her. When she tried to decipher something that her son had said to somebody else, her son Mustafa would tell her that she'd never understand, that there was no use in explaining it to her. She used to visit him at school, but he asked her never to return there because she didn't talk like all the other moms.

I missed the old neighborhood. I missed going casually from one place to another. I had decided to spend the holidays with my family. The roads were closed, but they opened the checkpoint on Christmas Eve. Crossing was only permitted on foot. We crossed. Karim and Lama walked close by my side. Each of them carried a small bag containing some notebooks, pens, and toys. Many people crossed in the same direction that day. Only a few people were headed toward the part of town we'd come from. Their bags showed that they intended to stay on the other side of Beirut and were unlikely to return anytime soon. They carried medium-sized suitcases and colorful plastic bags under their arms; the names of stores that sold clothes, perfumes, and foodstuffs were emblazoned on them, with telephone numbers, most of which no longer worked. The printing presses carried on as usual, cranking out bags with the same shape and the same address. Some of those addresses had become little more than piles, on top of which weeds had started to grow. The sun was rising, weak and wan. There was a biting cold in the shadowy places we passed through. "The sooner we get there, the sooner we'll be warm," I told the two of them. Karim asked me if Teta Laure had already decorated the tree. "I'm sure," I answered him.

This time, the Franciscan racetrack crossing was the open one. They were always changing which crossing would be open. Was there some reason they chose to open this one in particular or was it merely a coincidence? In between the two checkpoints, I stopped to catch my breath. The place was enormous. It was as though an ocean were held back by its high earthen walls. It was a different place to breathe. The sky was close but the horizon was wide. It felt like spring. The dark earth was muddy, shimmering in the sunlight. The stables with their thin tin roofs stood solitary. Large rocks and hunks of wood were placed on top of the tin sheets to prevent the wind from blowing them off. Not a single horse passed by or poked its head out from behind the stable door. I didn't hear any whinnying or trotting that might indicate the presence of life. I saw lots of people who didn't look like horses at all. "Mama, why do we always visit Teta Laure and Grandpa Khalil?" Lama asked. "Why don't they ever come to see us?"

Repetitive questions, children's voices, pedestrians, militiamen, checkpoints: Stop! Your

papers! Your things! Here! Move along!
Crossing. Clouds blocked out the sun for a few
moments. I pretended to be listening but I
wasn't. My mind never stopped racing. If only it
would stop, and Talal…? My eyes captured
everything: madness, violence, unforgiving
concrete vistas, buildings with bleeding walls,
evidence of the ongoing insanity as it sped
toward the abyss, possessions hanging out the
windows and the ripped-open walls. The eye
makes no mistakes. Only the heart does.

I heard my heavy breathing before I could hear
my own footsteps. I was exhausted. I remembered
that I had my two children with me. I looked
back. I sat down on the sidewalk among people
who were terrified of slowing down even for a
moment. I pressed on until I finally made it all
the way across. There were parked cars. "Taxi…
taxi… Madame?" "No, we want a service." We
occupied the entire back seat. I pulled a cigarette
out of my bag. I raised it to my mouth. I lit it,
trying to control the shaking of my hand. I
exhaled the cigarette smoke slowly and asked my
son to repeat the question he had just asked me,
the question I hadn't heard. Karim rolled down
the glass window, unhappy with the smoke
fumes. He stuck his head out the window and
tried to avoid making eye contact with me. He

wouldn't repeat his question but remained silent and angry, distant. I wasn't like this before, at least as I remembered myself and as Talal told me I once was. I couldn't hear Lama when she said something to me. It didn't even register that she was talking to me until she said something about how annoyed she was with me. Her words come out clear and harsh while she flailed her arms angrily. When I asked her, "What, what did you say?" she refused to respond and moved away from me, throwing her hands in the air then behind her, to make me understand that she no longer wanted anything, that she no longer wanted anything from me in particular. I told myself that I would have to focus better the next time she said something to me, or the next time Karim asked me for something. Sometimes I succeeded, but my success never lasted very long. I snapped back to my previous distracted-ness. The only time I found it possible to focus was when I held the transistor radio up to my ears and listened the news broadcast. Schools closed for long stretches of time. The shouting of children increased in the streets, at home, too. Andrea brought her two small children over. Languages get jumbled together when they're around: Andrea speaks German with them; Lama sings French songs her teacher taught her. The voices and names get all mixed up. I've discovered how the word "Yes" has a magical effect. I started using the word "Yes" to answer all of their endless questions.

"Can we play with the cushions to make a house?"

"Yes."

"Can we eat all the chocolate in the cupboard?"

"Yes."

"Can we go down to play in the building entryway?"

"Yes."

Karim opened the door. His chirping still echoes in my mind. I suddenly sensed that my son was opening the door and that he intended to go down to the building entrance. As though I'd just woken up, I heard the distant sounds of violence. I didn't know when it would descend on our street. I screamed out, "Where do you think you're going?" and demanded that Karim and his younger cousin close the door. Karim replied, "Downstairs," incredulous at the very question. "No, you are not going downstairs. You're staying right here!" Karim started to cry. "But you said I could." I ignored his crying and repeated my demand. I was firmly resolved to look Karim straight in the eye as though to tell him that I only agreed to let him go play in the street because of a momentary lapse of judgment. I would tell him that all of my attention was on him now. His whining wasn't going to work. I'd resist him and I wouldn't give in.

The war didn't change my family's home. It remained as it had always been, looking out over the town that had grown, sprawling toward the coast, its modern buildings built one on top of the other. These new buildings quickly filled with families that had come from various parts of the country. They found their new homes more secure than the old homes they had left behind. People always think like that when they move into a new home. They spread their possessions throughout the rooms of their new house. As time passes they have more houses but fewer possessions. These possessions become a burden for their owners to carry with them. Sometimes when they leave, therefore, they abandon some of their things in the places they're leaving. In their new homes, they forget that something terrifying is happening outside. When a window breaks for the first time, they are awestruck and surprised, as if discovering that their new home is also fragile, just like their old one, their old home that changed not only because of its gloomy vacancy or collapsed walls, but because of the new faces shacked up within.

The war didn't come to my family's home. It remained as it had always been, except it looked out onto a different scene than the one I was used to. The distant pine trees, which had once clung together and seemed high enough to touch the heart of the sky, disappeared. In the past, I could see them from the balcony of our house: a green blanket that the sky reclined on whenever it got tired. Tall buildings took their place. Our most pristine places were converted into sandlots where trucks rolled in and out. The scorched earth looked like the entrails of an eviscerated body. Some older buildings managed to save the sparse trees surrounding them. The trees next to our house remained as they had always been. They grew more solid, taller, and their branches blocked the eastern face of the house, making the balcony shadier and more intimate.

The sun had disappeared. Everyone was getting ready for Christmas Eve. Lama and Karim were playing with Janet's kids. They didn't see each other very often. I hadn't seen my sister's children for a very long time. They had grown up incredibly fast. Janet's husband arrived, his booming voice audible before his body even appeared at the door. He asked his driver to bring in the things from the car. He sat down next to my dad. The couch shook underneath him as he threw his weight on it. His face had grown rounder as he got fatter. Janet looked tiny beside him. When he put his arm around her, inviting her to get closer to him, I feared her bones might snap under his gigantic tree-trunk of an arm. My father was in his usual spot, fiddling with his ivory rosary when he wasn't playing back-gammon. I came to visit the house, to return to my home. Whenever I came back, my father was still in the same spot, as though he hadn't moved. The rosary, too, was still between his fingers as it had always been, except that its smooth, spherical ivory beads had become yellow from the constant touch of his fingers.

"Welcome, welcome," my sister's husband said to me. "How are things, good? Are you on strike again?" He always wants to have this never-ending conversation with me. I nodded my head in response to both questions: that is, things were good and we had been on strike the day before. My nod was not one of agreement; it was slow and short. "You people are always going on strike over something or other," he said, taking out a fat cigar from his pocket. I nodded at him, didn't say anything. I didn't ask who he meant by "you people." Did he mean the militias, the civilians, Muslims in general? Or perhaps he meant the Christians who dared to stay in West Beirut. My mother came and went from the kitchen to the living room, thanking her son-in-law for everything he had brought with him. "My son-in-law is such a big help," she said. "May God protect you." Then she thought better of what she had just said and looked sidelong at me, embarrassed, "And Talal, too." Your lifesaver, mother, has been smuggling imitation gasoline and young servant girls from the Philippines, I thought to myself, staring at my sister Janet's face.

She was looking at me, as if to say that the matter
was out of her hands. "He's my husband and I'm
used to him." She actually said that to me once.

I fled everyone, went in the bedroom to
unwind. The room was exactly as it had been
before Janet and I got married. The beds were
made but the bedspreads had been changed. My
mother had sewn new covers with daisies on
them in colors never seen in the wild.

The aromas of incense and flowers were
redolent in the church. The twelve chimes of
midnight heralding Jesus' birth hadn't been struck
yet. Voices intermingled as people congregated in
the hall. The sounds of coughing and children
crying rose in the air to touch the gray domed
ceiling. The chanting of hymns rang throughout
the church, passing the elevated apertures that
adorned the walls with their translucent stained
glass. Light from chandeliers was reflected off the
glass of the skylights, filtering pure orange light
through the colored glass. Children were crying
out of sleepiness and boredom. The place
amplified my feelings of loneliness. My mother
stood beside me. She sat down, stood up again.
When she kneeled and threw her head down
upon the wooden support, I noticed the amount
of gray hair on her head for the first time. The
deep lines in her neck and around her mouth had
grown thicker, but her body somehow managed
to retain its balance. My mother never once spoke

about feeling her age or about how she had grown old. It appeared as though she had never looked in the mirror and had never been afraid a day in her life. I kneeled beside her, the scents entering my nose. I felt dizzy for a moment. I closed my eyes, remembered a time when our bed was warm, when we, Talal and I, shared sadness and pleasure: How much more bearable life was back then. It occurred to me for a moment to leave everyone behind, to leave then, in that very moment—not the time that came before or the time that would come after—to take off running, to run as fast as my legs would carry me toward our house, our house where my room was and where Talal was. I would tell him how the pain had settled in me and how it had become worse than I could bear. I would tell him how I still dreamed of our first days together, how silence and doubt tore at my heart, at my soul. I would say everything and wait for him to say one word to me. Just one word. "What you said was beautiful, more beautiful than the life you're referring to. That's all well and good, but you're still just a little girl," I imagined him saying to me. I would bite down hard on my lip and the taste of blood would coat my tongue. I would ask myself what he wanted from me. Did he want me to stop dreaming and become a big girl just for him?

Whenever I visited my mother, it was as though I had just returned from a long voyage. I

would follow her around as she wandered
through the house, and ask her about things that
used to be there that I didn't see anymore. I asked
her about the wall that had been re-painted a
different color, about the oak wood table that
used to be in my room: Where had it gone? I had
carved my name and the name of a teacher of
mine whom I had a crush on into it when I was
fourteen. I went into every room, opened the
closets, rummaged through stuff, thumbed
through old albums, searched for my pictures,
pictures that united me with my family. I looked
everywhere. I went out to the backyard, to the old
seesaw. I saw our children sitting on it. The
walnut tree that once offered us shade had been
cut down, its trunk now dessicated. Its roots
stretched deep into the ground under the house;
the stump that remained was converted into a
table on which my mother would set the coffee
tray. I went back inside to rearrange the couches.
Then I lifted the edges of the small rugs that were
laid out on the ground, spreading them out to
straighten the dangling white cotton threads,
exactly as I used to when I came home from
college. In this way, I kept telling myself that I
was still a part of the house, that I had been
traveling but returned, that I had come back to
where I needed to be and where I was meant to
stay, as though I had never really left except for
some task that I'd quickly finished. I saw myself

hunting for moments long since passed, like one who catches butterflies in a net. How I longed to be a sly fox that at the end of the day could look back in satisfaction—stick out its tongue at the day it had lived through unscathed, without a trace of the deceit it had rolled around in, its perfect deceit. As soon as I entered my room to unwind, I'd rediscover the alienation I always felt in my mother's house. I stretched out on the bed that was once mine. The lingering cold under the covers surprised me. My feet got cold, so I rubbed them together to warm them up, but my body remained cold and the bed had been too long deserted, and released smells that had lain dormant in my deepest memory and were slow to awaken.

I visited my family. I left my home. Talk here, talk there: I could no longer stand hearing talk; talk aggravated the sickness in my soul; it was no longer possible for me to talk. I arrived at my family's house as though retracing my steps, then left. I went back to my own house. I decided to lock the door behind me, lie down on the sofa and stretch my legs out toward the wide door that led to the street. I extended my feet toward the outside, telling myself, "Don't worry, Lilian. Tomorrow is another day. Get up and stay strong." I expected to relax. I found the place filled with smells that weren't my own or my children's, smells that Talal's family had brought with them from their home. They brought them, spread them around my house like their possessions. The only place I encountered my own odor was in bed. The hajjeh boiled her clothes in water with a pinch of village soap. She added herbs I didn't know the names of to the rinse water. I lost track of my scent in both places. I could no longer guide myself. Smells have their locations, I like to say. The best places: the path between those two places, between my family's home and my own, where there are no houses, where there is no surplus of belonging, where faces are not defined by color or identity, where eyes speak another language, a language both patient and damning. Damning everything: geographical borders and history. Ahh, to stay there my whole life, suspended between those two places, claiming a third place that would be mine alone. But how could I do that when that third place was the most fragile, the most susceptible to fragmentation? The moment a shot was fired by a sniper moving along the rooftops near the checkpoint, my body tensed with fear.

My imagination was sparked on the road between the two places and wandered as far as it could. The distance grew longer as I was able to slow time down, proceeding however it suited me. I took a step, another, stopped. I retraced that step. I spun around like a bee unable to find the entrance to a hive, twisting around itself, until I couldn't take another step. I stepped forward on one foot, spun in a dance in which my body extended in every direction. Every dimension belonged to me, until suddenly all dimensions would vanish as a sniper's bullet whizzed by, the real owner of the place. It zoomed uninterested above my head. It penetrated all places and made me start to run, to run in a definite direction, one that would presumably lead somewhere I belonged. But the distance elongated, grew, and expanded toward the horizon. The horizon was where I yearned to be: where I belonged. I entered the neighborhood where my home awaited me, out of breath. I returned to Talal. I searched for a letter I desperately longed to read for a second time. I read him the letter, which was from Australia. Tony wrote, "I'm waiting for you with open arms." Here is someone, not Death, waiting for us with open arms. Can you believe it, Talal?

I was going to meet with the Australian consul on the twentieth of the next month, that is, in early spring. I prepared my papers and the children's papers. For some time, Talal had no longer been talking about leaving, as though he had forgotten we were getting ready to emigrate. This is desolate earth, I repeated to Talal as he struggled to change his clothes and button his own shirt with the help of his brother Abbas. Abbas came to take Talal back to his hometown for the commemoration of their grandfather's martyrdom. A new grave had been built for him out of tall marble, and flowers had been planted around it. "You have to come with me to see the consul. Can't you put off your visit to the South?" It had been years since Talal commemorated his grandfather's martyrdom. Why was he going now, and why did Abbas seem so enthusiastic about it? "Why don't *you* put off going to Cyprus?" Abbas asked me aggressively. "Doesn't this man mean anything to you? Besides, can't you just send your papers to Damascus? That would be easier for you and for us. Then you could go and be home on the same night." I told him I wanted to go to Cyprus. I went out to the balcony and foggy clouds appeared before my eyes. I wasn't going to cry this time. To hell with Talal and Abbas, to hell with martyrdom and commemoration.

Talal busied himself getting ready for the commemoration ceremony, which Abbas had organized in cooperation with the Party. In the past, Talal's father used to come, pressuring Talal to come with him and take part in the ceremony. Talal would refuse, saying he was too busy. Then for many years the family stopped honoring the tradition because they were too busy with other things.

What caused Talal to change like this? What brought about this desire to talk about his grandfather? Or this desire to know his origins and birthplace, the details of his grandfather's life and the life of his grandfather's last wife, who didn't have any children? What was there for me in such a search through the void? I had come to see Lama and Karim as the present as well as whatever came after. While Talal was busy rewriting his commemoration address, I asked him why we search for our identity among the dead, why this search always takes us back into the past. I knew that to search somewhere else, in that moment in particular, would require extraordinary courage, courage Talal no longer possessed. I would have said that what he was doing might still be good for him, but I was sure he was adding yet another level to our estrangement. Talal stopped answering me when I spoke to him. He started getting angry whenever I brought up leaving. He would say how our children were no worse off than the children of many other families, families that had no choice but to stay. What sort of staying was this he talked about, staying only to conjure the spirits of the dead?

The night we left for Cyprus, we had to re-cross the checkpoint, where my sister Janet waited for us with a childhood friend George. He was traveling on the same ship as us, and then continuing on to Canada. He had emigrated ten years earlier and acquired Canadian citizenship.

When Talal dropped us as close as possible to the checkpoint, Abbas was driving, and I started to imagine that Talal was coming with us after all. It seemed as though he wasn't sure what he was going to do after I left. He was trying to fill the gaps of silence in the car with questions like, "Did you forget anything?" "Where will you stay in Cyprus?" I didn't feel much like talking. I found myself relying heavily on one phrase—*inshallah*—when he told me to come back safely. He bid me farewell with a quick wave, saying that he might be heading to the South the next day. I moved away from the car, Lama and Karim lugging suitcases behind them. I stopped for a moment to look back at where we'd gotten out. I saw Abbas trying to back the car up; beside him I could make out Talal watching us. Their features started to shrink and grew fainter as the car moved back toward where it had come from. When I started to raise my hand and wave, Lama grabbed my hand and told me to keep moving; Karim added that there was someone waiting for us so we needed to hurry. I breathed deeply and slowly, as though repressing a last desire to return to the place I had left behind. I inhaled again, telling myself it was a beautiful thing to know there was someone waiting for you on the other side of the city.

Nothing remained of the George I had once known except for his brown eyes and the pleasant smile I had always liked. His hair had thinned out and his face seemed much wider than I remembered it; he had combed a small tuft of hair forward in order to cover up his bald spot. He extended his hand to shake mine but seemed unsure of himself, as though meeting me for the first time. But our conversation eliminated the hesitation in his voice and eyes. George, my friend who I hadn't seen for more than ten years—how I'd missed him and how violent our last meeting had been, much like the war that broke out at the same time. His family used to spend summers in our town. After the war started, they ended up staying there year round.

The sea was calm that evening during our journey to the island. The cabins were packed with families leaving Beirut to wait for visas there. In the small cabin, Karim took out a book decorated with colorful pictures. He sat with Lama on the narrow bed. He flipped through the pages, rubbing his weary eyes, and fell asleep. I peered through the tiny window and saw the growing distance between the coast and our ship. The deep waves the ship left on the surface of the water were quickly swallowed by the sea and disappeared.

I found George sitting at the restaurant bar on the ship's top floor. "You're bearing your own cross now. I made a trip just like yours ten years ago when I first wanted to emigrate to Canada," George said as I took a seat next to him. "You didn't waste your time waiting," I said. I looked at him and thought, My God, how we'd changed. How we used to fight back at the outbreak of the war. I got so angry whenever he talked to me about politics just to provoke me. We were enemies but neither emerged victorious. Rather, we were both losers until the bitter end. Now, after all that bloodshed and all the years we had lost, the conflict had become bound up with our very lives. As though the violence, which had dragged on for years and lasted far too long, held our personal conflict together, refining it, making it more tolerable than it was before. That's war, my friend: the most despicable way of disagreeing. "Did we really need all that violence?" I asked him, after we'd descended the stairs to the lower floor where the sleeping cabins were located.

When we embraced in his cabin, next door to the children's cabin, his breath was perfumed and warm like the breath of people I love. In that moment we seemed to be reclaiming a world we had lost a long time before, the absence of which had always tortured us, the kind of torture that doesn't subside until we prepare to make peace with our own bodies. "You. I want you," he told me as he squeezed my hand. Pain coursed through my fingers like rushing water, like a wind shaking my foundations, leaving smooth earth in its wake. We made peace with our bodies. So why did I, in that moment, feel I was tilting at windmills, not finding peace, a poker player who knows there is only loss at the end of the round, but who plays her hand anyway, out of her passion for taking risks.

From the narrow bed we lay on, I could see scattered orange clouds float past. They seemed so close, as though all I would have to do to grab them would be reach through the circle of glass. A million stars lit the vast sky. Shooting stars zoomed by, leaving streaks behind them that sparkled, then died with stunningly brutal familiarity.

The Egyptian-born Greek woman I used to stay with whenever I was in Cyprus questioned me about the yellowness of my face, my skinniness. Lama and Karim went out to the garden the moment we arrived. Maria hadn't changed since the last time I saw her except that she had gained some weight. She still spent her time watching Egyptian movies and weeping. She lifted the glasses from her face and wiped her tears, saying how she still hadn't forgotten her childhood and adolescence in Alexandria. I was worn out the day I arrived. George checked into a hotel not far from the furnished apartments Maria managed, the only building she still owned since the island had been partitioned; all of her other properties were located on the northern, Turkish side. "No, you're not going to sleep just yet. Stay and have lunch with us," she said, grabbing my hand and continuing a conversation with an American woman who was staying with her. Mrs. Took was married to a Lebanese-American man from Bsharré, from the Tawq family. He worked at the American Embassy in Morocco. When Maria told her I was moving to Australia for good, she expressed sympathy and asked, with extreme naïveté, "Why can't the Lebanese just get along with each other? And the Maronites, who are they anyway? Are they Muslims or Christians?" "They're Christians, my dear," Maria answered her, laughing before adding, "Yes, it's a shame they can't all get along. I heard that religious men there are calling for an end to the fighting, even the Mufti." "The Mufti… what's the Mufti?" Mrs. Took asked without much interest. "He's the Patriarch of Islam," Maria responded, switched off the television and pivoted her exhausted body, moving slowly and heavily toward the kitchen.

We spent ten days on the island. I had to fill out new forms because of Talal's absence from the interview. The woman who filled out the remainder of our documents for me whispered that there might be new problems waiting in the consul's office since we had already turned in a different emigration application with Talal present. Besides, he no longer wanted to emigrate. "Maybe it's best if you change the word 'married' to 'separated' in that box at the top of the first page," the woman suggested, staring at me with beady eyes. "Separated, divorced, whatever," I said disinterestedly. "The visa is the important thing. When will I have it anyway?"

The consul bombarded me with questions. Why was I traveling? Where was my husband? Why had he changed his mind and what did his accident have to do with it? Were my life and the lives of the children at risk? In the marital status box, I wrote "separated" instead of starting a new application. I waited for my brother Tony to fax a sponsorship letter to the embassy declaring that he would bear responsibility for my two children and me.

George rented a small car. It didn't take long for us to cover all the Greek areas of the island. Spring ignited the earth into a thousand colors. Their war was clean and light, George said, as we passed the old airport, where the runway had become the dividing line between the two sides of the island. The residents had grown accustomed to partition and built another airport in a different city that overlooked the sea.

"Let's celebrate the next few years," I said to George after emerging from the embassy for the last time, carrying entry visas on our three passports. I'll leave for Beirut tomorrow morning. George will leave for Canada that very evening, where his Canadian family is waiting for him. "Will we ever see each other again?" he asked me. "Let's leave our meetings to fate," I told him. I knew that I was only going back to Beirut so I could scrounge up enough money, as fast as possible, to buy plane tickets and leave again. I would sell the piano, the only thing I owned, which I no longer needed.

In the evening, Maria sat down beside me on the big sofa after turning on the TV to watch one of her Egyptian films. Karim opened his Arabic textbook. The book looked shiny and clean and a light odor wafted out of it, the smell of libraries and printing presses. "B," said Karim, "B as in Beirut." "Yes, B as in Beirut," I replied. "B, Beirut, *bayt*," Karim said. Yes, I whispered to myself, Beirut: fragments of home.

Warda

In the end, only a few women dared to stay in the bomb shelter. When the doorman went to the South, I hoped he would never come back. I started to take pleasure in going up to my apartment and behaving as if I owned the whole world. I went back to arranging the couches however I liked; I rearranged them and hung my clothes up to cover all the windows. The doorman who used to live in the dark room next to the elevator would grumble and threaten that he could bring some young men from the Party headquarters near our building anytime he wanted. He would tell me that he couldn't get any sleep because of the racket I made all night. He was a liar. I was just redecorating: I mopped the floor and scrubbed the walls whenever there was water; I picked the books up off the table, the dull black Formica table, one at a time and wiped off the dust. How could so much dust have accumulated overnight? I scoured the cover of each book with all my might, books that Rashad had brought back when he was still able to get in to Lebanon, books that stayed in their place, books that I would clean every day but never open. I cleaned them, saying how the next time I wouldn't find even one speck of dust, how they would stay clean forever. But I was always disappointed the next morning. It's strange how dust particles seem to accumulate at the speed of light, piling up like seconds or hours, like time itself.

Rashad would read those books whenever he came to Lebanon. Last time, he wasn't allowed in and was sent straight from the Beirut airport back to the Gulf. I sat on the loveseat facing the big couch. I talked with guests who were sitting on it and said whatever had to be said on such occasions. Sometimes I could hear their answers; sometimes they would just disappear inexplicably. I became upset with them for leaving without saying goodbye. Then darkness crept in and filled the room. I discovered that my legs had completely fallen asleep and that I was sprawled out on the sofa without a blanket. I shivered from the cold slinking in through the broken window behind me. I tried to stand up, to go over and close the window. I told myself they had left it open on purpose, even though they knew I was extremely sensitive to the cold wind that whipped in from outside. In the bedroom with the curtains drawn, sleep took me by surprise. Inside, it seemed like night. From time to time, rose colors passed through a narrow slit at the curtain's edge. The light cast a small rectangle that stopped just before the leg of the bed.

When I first came back from the Gulf, candles used to annoy me. I couldn't sleep next to them because, back there, I had grown accustomed to sleeping with the whir of the air conditioning throughout the night. Then I got used to the candles. I started leaving lit candles scattered all along the bedroom floor, near the walls so that their light wouldn't extend through the apartment's openings and no one would be able to see me from outside; that way, neither the doorman nor the youth at the Party headquarters would know whether I was still awake. If they heard a noise, I would protest that it hadn't come from my apartment. It's true that I shut the curtains but shrapnel found a way to leave gaping holes in them. I hung the laundry up to dry in the living room. I bought a laundry line, hammered a nail into the wall on one side of the room and a second on the other, stretched the rope out in front of the wide curtains and hoisted it up. I stood on the chair I had brought in from the kitchen so I could hang up the wet clothes. I

wouldn't have to go out on the balcony anymore.
The dim candlelight protected me from everyone's prying.

The only window in the room looked out over
the backyard. That place that was once so
important to me had become useless, shut tight
ever since I had returned. The curtains were
drawn, too. I always knew where my room was in
the building and where my building was in the
neighborhood. I had perfected my sense of
direction, and I was always able to tell which side
we were on. The sun was no longer my fixed point
of reference; it seemed absent altogether. The sea
was the only thing that didn't change on me. I
closed my eyes in my cramped little room. At that
moment, the sea appeared before me and I
imagined it close by, so close I could rest my
elbows on it. Then I grew, bit by bit, and drifted
off in all three directions. I knew the streets, the
buildings, the alleyways and the roads, even the
cart sellers who had sprouted up ever since
downtown disappeared. I knew all of the distances
separating me from the coast. I started out from
the massive building that blocked my view, turned
toward the Damascus road, then onto Beshara al-
Khoury Street, descending toward the city center.
My imagination was dashed on the rooftops of
apartment buildings and swam across an ashen
cement desert to reach the edges of the blue. I
always did love the color blue.

I memorized the dimensions of my apartment. When I was done cleaning, I would close my eyes and guess where everything was. I would close my eyes and stand far away from the sofa. Then I'd declare where the television was. I'd start to walk, a few paces toward the television. Once I found it, I'd be pleased with myself and then quiz myself on where something else was. Sometimes I'd take my hanging clothes off the line in the living room. I'd take them down with my eyes still shut. I knew every piece of clothing from the feel of its material. I knew exactly what they were. I'd fold them, bring them into the bedroom, and put them away in drawers. I enjoyed playing this game. When Josefa arrived, I would ask her to hide. So she would hide in secluded and strange places, but I found her by the trail of her scent. I remembered her scent well, the regularity of her breathing. I would find her quickly and call out her name. When she pretended not to hear me and kept hiding, I would draw in close and wrap my arms around her. Josefa laughed like someone caught unawares.

My heart quaked at the impending sounds of death. The wooden front door shuddered and creaked. The wind carried sounds of horror through all the rooms of my house. It penetrated the pores of my skin, my skin that had turned yellow and would only regain its natural color when I took refuge in bed and covered up my entire body.

Before, I used to go downstairs twice a day and walk my dog Blackie. But after he disappeared, there wasn't any need to go out anymore. I knew exactly who had kidnapped him, but I would never dare ask him about it. During the few days following Blackie's disappearance, I would wake up in a panic, imagining he was in bed with me and that his head was next to mine, that he was burying his nose in my hair and slopping his tongue across my face. I used to hear his howling, but became convinced after a while that those noises were from some stray dog searching for food among the trash heaps of our dark city.

It was easy for me to figure out that no one was living across from me in those cement buildings with the high walls that suffocated me. Their apartments were totally empty. The flowers and plants, scattered on the desolate balconies, had recently grown yellow and desiccated. This was the most compelling evidence that the apartments were empty. I would stand near the corner of the room, pull aside the holey curtain and lean backward, pressing my head against the wall, straining ever closer to peer through the translucent plastic I'd affixed to the window to replace the broken glass. I would stare for a long time: no one there. If there had been someone there, they would have watered their flowers, fixed the holes in their damaged windows. But what if there were someone, someone just like me, too frightened to step out onto the balcony? Maybe they weren't staying inside their rooms because of the almost constant bombardment, but because they had lost any desire to see what was going on outside. Or perhaps they stopped watering their flowers because of the water shortage. They might drink, cook their food, wash their clothes, and then use the old laundry water in their toilet. To have running water at all, like watering the flowers, had become a real luxury.

Josefa told me about the arrival of many new families in our neighborhood. It's amazing I never noticed them. How could I have not bumped into one of their children playing and shouting in the streets? How could I not have seen them all around me, taunting me with their childish songs like "Here comes Miss Crazyhair" or throwing a ball at me as I walked by? Josefa would accompany me and scream at them, raising her hand and threatening to hit them so they scattered and took off. I often heard voices rising from the street under my balcony, but I would convince myself that they were voices from distant neighborhoods, echoing between the buildings. "Miss Crazyhair," my husband's sister Najla would repeat, laughing wickedly as she gazed down at me from the balcony. When I got home, I would gather all my hair up into a twist and clasp it with a black barrette.

On my large balcony, I had lots of flowers, sprouting high enough to reach the balcony above: tall gardenias and jasmine. I used to put a chair out there and sit beside them. Their leaves shielded me from the sunlight. As the gardenias and the jasmine plants grew, my stomach distended with them. The jasmine shaded me and shaded my daughter, swimming in my amniotic fluid. "I'll stay here," I whispered to myself with an inner strength that prevailed over my fragility. But things changed rapidly. They changed rapidly and I took shelter inside the apartment, no longer going out onto the balcony except for brief moments. "Come quick!" That's all Rashad ever said on the phone. I opened the suitcases; I closed the suitcases. I went back. Then I hurried off once again. The situation was good; no, the situation was bad. I traveled once again even as my stomach was growing, becoming a solid dome that thrust itself into the world like a boulder atop a mountain. Come quick, he said. I returned to the Gulf, to my house that had no balcony, no jasmine.

When I went back to the Gulf, my husband's sister Najla stayed in my apartment. I came back years later to find all of the pots empty except for dead, dried-out soil. When I told Najla how sad I was about my plants, she shrieked, "You wish I had watered your flowers when I didn't even have enough water to wash with! You all deserve far worse than war in your country, let me tell you." I told her she could have brought water from the doorman's room because his was the only room that ever got any, that it didn't get drawn up to the water tanks on the roof. In my heart, I was scared of her being there with me and I thought being alone would probably be safer. I knew that if I, like those flowers, got thirsty, she wouldn't spare me one drop of water. I didn't tell her what I was thinking, muttering something else instead. I asked myself what would happen if I replaced my sentence with someone else's. Perhaps I would appear more rational, perhaps more insane. But I knew full well that, like all other human beings, I was incapable of saying what really had to be said or of undoing what had already come out of my mouth.

Many things had changed since my last visit. On one of the balconies of the white building that had been built even as they tore down others, I could see a wooden cage with metal bars that had been painted white and decorated with blue beads. The cage was wide and round and had a domed roof. There were two lovebirds inside, and every morning, a white-haired man who was at least sixty years old would carry the cage out onto the balcony and hang it from an iron hook in the ceiling. Then he would open the cage door to pet the two birds and talk to them. His lips moved and his eyes shone. He cleaned the floor of the cage, changed the water and sprinkled some grain and hemp seeds. He was alone. One day at sunset, I noticed he hadn't come out on the balcony to take the cage in. The cage was hanging there, swaying in the breeze. It rained that evening, the bombs poured down, and the night was long. The cage was still hanging there. I could see it right there in front of me. Everything became quiet. The color of the cage blended in with the color of the building. The wall was filthy and the city air was heavy with dust and death. I was alone, too.

When the bombardment intensified, Maha would come down to sleep next to me. In the shelter, her chest constricted until she nearly suffocated. I always waited for her, and every time, I imagined that her presence alone could shatter my severe solitude. Sometimes I simply longed to embrace her, to sleep the entire night clinging to her. We wouldn't be afraid of the bombing or of being alone. I used to open the photo album for her, inviting her to look at pictures of my daughter from the day she was born until the present. I hadn't seen Sara for two years, ever since I left the Gulf and came back to Lebanon. She was eight years old. Every summer

I wanted to bring her here, but Rashad forbid me and refused to pay for a plane ticket.

I can still hear my daughter's voice speaking that country's dialect. I can also hear her speaking English. I would tell Najla how my daughter was still with us, and she said, "Really, you've lost it." You've lost it, why did she always say that to me, and why did the doorman's wife say the same thing? One day, I called her husband up and gave him some money to go down and buy me some oven-roasted chicken. When he came back, he gave me the chicken and the change. I left the money in his hand, the chicken too. I told him to take Blackie down to the street and feed him the chicken. The doorman looked me square in the eye. He couldn't believe what was happening. Then he grabbed the leather collar wrapped around Blackie's neck and took off running down the stairs, the dog racing behind him in great anticipation even though he had never liked the doorman. Whenever he rang the doorbell, Blackie would sit behind the door and growl angrily. He knew him by smell. He used to bark before I even opened the door. The doorman stopped in front of his door and told his wife, "Look at this, can you believe she wants me to feed this to the dog." "Give it to me! Give it to me!" the woman commanded. "We'll feed it to the children. Whatever's left over will be enough for the dog." The woman took the warm chicken and repeated, "That woman's lost it, I swear to God, she's lost it."

I was convinced that Najla was lying to me and that she was conspiring with her brother to keep me from my daughter. Maha used to look at me and I couldn't tell whether she even heard what I was saying to her. Her eyes were vacant and I couldn't decipher them. I was angry when she asked me if I had been going to see Dr. Azuri. Had she begun to hate me? Was she just like Najla? But all I could say was that it was very kind of her to ask. Whenever Josefa went to visit her friends in East Beirut, Maha would take me into the bathroom and help me take my clothes off, pour water on my back and rub her warm hand up and down. She scrubbed my back with the sponge and washed my hair with shampoo. I used to close my eyes and wish that Maha would let her warm hands linger on my body even longer. She used to offer me clean clothes. She never seemed disgusted by me the way Najla always was. She hugged me and brushed my hair. Sometimes she even surprised me by buying things I desperately needed, that I had neglected to buy for a long time. I used to wake up and say that I was going to take a shower that day, but I couldn't even muster up the strength to get out of bed. The entire day passed and the sun disappeared, leaving me cold and postponing my shower for one more day. The first beam of sunlight that streamed in through the tattered curtains would rejuvenate me and invigorate the blood in my veins. I used to look at pictures of my daughter Sara and feel as though I was losing my memory. I no longer remembered how I had spent those eight years with her. I remembered the moment she was born very well, how I cried when I first laid eyes on her. I was like someone who had been emptied of a love that had once filled her. The moment I left the house, she wrapped her arms around my neck and wouldn't let go. My husband Rashad whisked me off to the airport. I remembered how she didn't want me to leave. On the plane, I could still picture Sara's hair: wavy and golden like her father's. That was the only thing she inherited from him. I got up from my seat in the back of the plane and walked down the aisle toward first class. I brushed aside the orange curtain with my hand. I was certain that Sara would be there waiting for me. I didn't know how she would appear to me. Or maybe she didn't even know that I was on the same flight with her, or… or… I glanced around me… scanned each and every face… searched among the seats… under the seats… above the seats… Sara wasn't there… she had disappeared… disappeared like a magician's handkerchief… I looked again… but I had seen her… her hair

from behind… her wavy golden hair. The hair she
had inherited from her father.

I was terrified of being alone and of getting old
before I would have the chance to see my
daughter again. My memory only knew two
states: a death-like fear, a fear of everything, a fear
so paralyzing it kept me in bed for days on end,
leaving a sharp pain in the pit of my stomach; or
intense pleasure that spread an insatiable passion
throughout my body that could only be compared
to the passion of life, the pleasure that inhabited
me while I was pregnant with Sara. Between
those two extremes, my memory was blank.
Everything passed me by vaguely, almost without
having any effect on me whatsoever. Maybe that's
just life, I thought. Maybe there's no point in
trying to stop it or trying to change it. At least
that's what I said when Rashad first came to visit
my brother. They were friends from working
together in the Gulf. Then he and I became
friends and my brother's wife invited me to hang
out with them. When he stayed for dinner, my
mother purposefully began to heap praise on me
in front of him. I could sense a certain mutual
understanding: my brother and Rashad had
worked together and were going to become
related through marriage. My mother and my
brother's wife exaggerated, describing me as

perfect and skilled in housework. At that dinner, I understood from my mother's eyes how much she wanted me to keep silent, not to move from my place. But I couldn't bear it. The hands of madness returned to press down on my body. The spasms tore into me. They began from the bottom of my feet, rising to my thighs and into my midsection. I started biting my lips, biting hard so that the cry of pain wouldn't escape me, so that it would get caught in the depths of my throat and stop right there. But I couldn't control my body's shaking any longer. My brother looked over at my face anxiously and suddenly got up to invite Rashad out to the garden, to show him the colorful flowers my mother had planted.

We were engaged for one week, which we spent shopping for a trousseau. Then Rashad went back to work in the Gulf. I joined him two months later. Once there, I had to get to know the man who had become my husband, to grow accustomed to his presence, to seeing him in my bed, to feeling him on top of me. I didn't know how a woman was supposed to feel with a man in her bed. He seemed like a father to me somehow, maybe because he was twenty years older than me. Naïvely, I had thought that I would sleep in his arms, that he would stay by my side all night, tenderly caressing my hair until I fell asleep. My home was fully furnished when I arrived. He had even picked out the sheets on our bed. I didn't have to do anything. I would leave the television on all day because I was all by myself and didn't have anyone to talk to. After a while, I started getting headaches that lasted several days, and I went back on the pills that Dr. Azuri had prescribed for me in Lebanon. The apartment I lived in only had one small balcony, just off the kitchen, a balcony looking out onto the walls of a garden fenced in by three buildings, including the one I lived in. I would turn off the television and open the balcony door to get some fresh air. Then I'd retrace the same steps back inside. I remembered that I was in a foreign country where I didn't know anyone, where I couldn't even drive a car because I was a woman. Sometimes I'd consider opening the living room window, fantasizing that it might be a door leading to a balcony. The hot wind, dry and sandy, scorched me, so I closed the window quickly and turned the television back on.

When I got pregnant, my headaches went away and my health improved. I felt a childlike joy and spent my days shopping for the new baby, passing the time getting the baby's room ready. I didn't have any friends. We used to spend Fridays with my brother and his wife. My brother would drive Rashad's car and carry the picnic supplies. Rashad was always in charge and my brother listened to everything he said with what seemed like artificial interest. I knew that there was something going on between my husband and my brother's wife, Huda. She'd wrap her arms around her husband's body and kiss him loudly on the mouth. She'd remain like that for a few moments, looking at my husband with brazen lasciviousness, batting her eyes at him. I was stricken with a passing dizziness. I didn't know what I was supposed to do in such moments. Was I just supposed to keep watching her, pretending to make lunch?

My brother's wife was a beautiful woman, very beautiful. I was jealous of her. I would have loved to be like her: to doll myself up every morning and come out of my room knowing exactly what I wanted from my day and exercising a certain control over my house and my family. Her presence was oppressive and powerful. When she talked, everyone listened, although I always thought that she only ever had trivial things to say. I tried emulating her, but I couldn't stand it. I did myself up for one day but got so annoyed that I nearly suffocated on the next day. I went back to letting my hair down as I always had, and removed the polish from my fingernails. I knew that Rashad wanted her. I could read it in his eyes. I could see it in their stolen glances, their impatience, their ardent desire to be together. Sometimes, I'd almost say I even understood Rashad. I understood him when he lusted after Huda. She was beautiful. I never once denied myself the opportunity to rub my hand across her bare upper arm, to comment on how smooth her skin was. I didn't care whether her skin was actually smooth, but I was consumed by this devilish desire to know the essence of the infatuation that had taken over Rashad and motivated him to caress her arm. Huda never responded to me, moving away instead by suddenly jerking backward.

I didn't have to wait long until I saw him reach his hand out under the table and fondle her, until I knew there was something going on between them. I could sense it from the beginning. I wasn't jealous, but furious at this woman my brother had trusted. I thought, what if my brother knew what was going on? How could all of that go on right in front of him without his suspecting something? I looked at him. He cast a short sideways glance at the two of them before turning his head aside. He made some meaningless small talk. I felt as though I was losing my memory whenever I looked at a picture of my daughter. For a few moments, I would even forget her name. What was her name? I wondered. That she was still my daughter and that she was the most beloved creature to my heart never once escaped my mind. Then my memory would return once again. I could remember her name. I would repeat it several times in a row so that my memory wouldn't betray me again.

I was so frightened by the last bombing that I almost swallowed my tongue. Maha grabbed me and pulled me up against the wall. We couldn't make it down to the shelter. Maha couldn't carry me, not even with Najla's help. But when Josefa came, she carried me easily. While Josefa was carrying me, I felt as light as a feather. This had happened to me before. I was used to seeing the *djinn* and the two women grew used to my condition. My eyes remained open. I was looking at them constantly and I refused to let Najla touch me. I was terrified when she approached me and I screamed from the intensity of the pain. She swore to God that she hadn't touched me yet, that her hands were far away from me. She started nervously repeating that I was mad. But she was hurting me, burning me. When I woke up the next day, I saw a blue spot spreading all over my body. I knew that it was the devil's handiwork, that she alone was the reason all of this was happening to me. When Abu Ali came back to make peace with her, I breathed a sigh of relief and thought that she was finally going to leave me this time, maybe for good, but she came back just two months later. I was afraid of her return and she became even moodier and more nervous than she had been before. I made Maha swear that she would never leave me alone with Najla. I started sleeping with Maha in my room, leaving the other room to Najla.

I remember the picture of the Virgin Mary that hung in the salon of our large house back in town. My mother used to take it down twice a year: once before Christmas and once before Easter. She would take it down, shake off the dust and polish the glass. She wouldn't put it down on the table, but keep it in her hand and wipe the glass with eau de cologne. She'd talk to it, kiss it, then hang it up again. The picture of the virgin would come off the wall twice a year and then be returned to its place. There was a tremendous explosion early one evening. The picture fell and the wall collapsed on top of it. My mother screamed as she ran toward us. My father's body crashed onto the floor. My mother kneeled by his body, laid out near the threshold. "I knew this was going to happen," she said. "I sensed it the last time I touched the picture." I was still young then and I had opened the door for him. He had only one more step to go when we heard the explosion. It sent me flying from where I was onto the couch in the living room. Just one more step inside would have saved his life from the projectile that destroyed our house's outer walls. My father's death had saved my life, that's what my mother said. My mother's words echoed in my head. She said that my father's death had saved my life, but it couldn't save me from the pain that devoured me from within, that had been part of me ever since his death. Searing pain: like being impaled on barbecue skewers. I screamed and ground my teeth together from the pain that started somewhere deep in back and spread outward, rising to my neck, expanding throughout my entire body. My limbs tingled and my legs went numb. My mother squeezed one hand as my brother squeezed the other, trying to keep my hands away from my face, but usually I was stronger than both of them. I clawed at my face with my fingernails and bit my tongue, trying to taste the blood I swallowed whenever I wasn't screaming. I woke up to find my robe torn. My mother cursed the hour I was born. She pressed her palms against her temples and shook her head violently, saying that I had torn all of my robes.

We stayed in my uncle's house for two weeks while he rebuilt the walls of our house. But my mother wanted to leave. "I lost a husband and I almost lost a daughter," she said. She wanted to go to Beirut. My uncle couldn't stop her. My brother wanted to stay in town. He started crying when my mother scolded him or asked him to help carry what household supplies remained, to place them in the back of the small truck. My brother was small, too small to get in my mother's way or to make her stay.

We settled in the city, near the Daraj Ja'ara staircase. A relative of my mother who had lived in the city for years found us a place on the ground floor of an old three-story stone building.

The building entrance looked right out onto the stairs. I loved our new place even though it was small and was always dark inside, which meant we had to leave the electric lights on all the time. Only the kitchen ever got any natural light, which streamed in through the door and the window that overlooked the backyard. I was secretly happy that our kitchen was so spacious and well-lit, but only because my mother spent more than half of her time in it. Maybe that was where the doorman used to live. Nothing about the behavior of the other tenants seemed to change once we had arrived and settled into the apartment. They went on chucking their garbage from their balconies, out their windows. It flew through the air and piled up in the backyard garden where my mother had planted roses of various colors and salad greens. At first, my mother tried calling out to stop them. She told them that we were the new tenants and that the garbage fell on our heads when we sat out in the garden. The residents didn't give up their tradition, even as my mother's calm words, after some time, turned into curses and insults.

I remember all that very well. Remembrance is alive somewhere in my mind. I remember that something between sleep and wakefulness used to burn me up inside, preventing me from moving. I used to have trouble breathing because of what felt like a heavy weight on my chest, a weight that smelled like the locked places deep inside me. I would feel pain in the lower half of my body before getting dizzy and passing out. I used to turn away from it, reciting the name of the Virgin Mary. It craned its neck and relaxed its hands when I prayed for peace to be upon her. It moved away from me. My entire face was shriveled and wet, my body dripping with warm sweat. The virgin had always come to my rescue. Sometimes I would call out for her, pleading for her mercy so that I might actually see her. She'd appear to me in those moments of my deepest pain and terror. My body ached and cried out. I knew that my body was in pain when it started to shudder and thrash about. Pain flashed like an arrow of fire. It burrowed inside my head and I couldn't think; it caused me to lose the ability to focus. I forgot everything: my name and the names of my family members. I was terrified of these moments of forgetfulness. I looked at my family for a few moments. I recognized all of their faces. I stared at one face for a long time; some of the faces reminded me of the fear that I had tried to forget ever since my childhood. Some of the faces got mixed together and became a single, recurring face, a face that I knew, that I knew well but was trying to forget. It was the face of my father. No… No… My father had been dead for a long time, since the picture of the virgin fell from the wall. He had been just one step away from survival. The virgin didn't grant him survival. She wanted to save me and me alone, to save me from the wall and from him. From him? Who was he anyway? My father? No... No... My father had been dead for a long time. It was the *djinn* that assaulted my body and weighed heavily atop me like a cold, metallic spacecraft, like a burden that prevented me from breathing, that renewed my searing pain. My father was almost able to enter the house that night, but the virgin fell and made the wall come down after her.

I lost the ability to pronounce words. A great invisible power assaulted me and the name of the virgin rang from my mouth: a single name, repeated, pure. She comes to me on rare occasions dressed in a sky blue that reflects off her face and her eyes, which sometimes looked blue and sometimes light brown. I would say, "Please, virgin, rescue me. I know you're testing me but this is more than I can stand!"

Josefa took me to the Dikwaneh neighborhood, where the Virgin Mary was said to have appeared. I had waited a long time to see her. I knew that one day she would satisfy my longing. I prayed to her and asked her to appear, even just once. Josefa held my hand when we got out of the taxi in the

Salomé neighborhood and crossed the roundabout. We entered a narrow alley where a crowd was milling. Night had fallen. A soft breeze kicked up the smell of wet earth and spread it through the air. Mud covered the feet of the supplicants and believers. I stood at the back of the crowd. They were transfixed, looking at her, at what they could make out of her recognizable figure, bathed in divine blue light. But she wasn't looking at them; she was looking at me. She searched for me among all of them and, when she finally saw me, fixed her gaze on my face. Warmth rose from my face like smoke. My heart began to beat like a prisoner begging to be released and my chest rose and fell. My heartbeat grew louder, began ringing in my ears. Then I heard the sound of my own voice, I heard my sobbing rising from deep inside me and overflowing from my mouth. My sobbing spilled out continuously, drenched further by the water streaming from my eyes. I saw her. I tried to move closer, to pierce the crowd, to try to touch her body. I reached toward her, but the cold glass refracting her light stopped my outstretched hand and kept me from reaching her. Was all of this crying necessary in order for her to hear me, all this pain, all the torment that remains bored into my skin? It penetrated deep inside me, absorbed like semen. For a few moments she had looked at me, but I was suddenly no longer able to see her face. Why did I see her more clearly in my dreams? Why could I no longer see her face or the color of her eyes? Was it because of all the people around me, because of all the sounds and smells of their breathing? I know that she doesn't like crowds, but she looked at me, and I heard her say, "I am with you: Do not be afraid. Stay as you are!" I cried more. "Holy Mary, Mother of God, deliver me from these torments. Give me back my daughter!" I could hear my voice echo. Then the words of the Virgin: "Sara is here in Beirut." "It's Najla, Najla!" I screamed to Josefa. She's the one who kidnapped her. I knew it all along.

I'm afraid of getting old, afraid of being alone. When she finally sees me, Sara won't even recognize that I'm Warda, Warda who suffered to give birth to her. Will she know me when she sees me? Will she rub her face in my bosom and breath in my scent like she did when she was a child? She used to close her eyes and I would listen to her last words—that she loved my smell—before falling asleep. Does she miss my smell, or does the smell of the Filipina maid cover up any trace of me?

The money I used to receive every month lasted no longer than a week. I don't know how Josefa managed to get the food that she brought me from her rations. I didn't eat that food. Instead, I sold the cans to the shopkeeper at the end of the street. With what little money I got

from him, I bought coffee and cigarettes.
Sometimes I would hide a pack of cigarettes
under my bed and ask Lilian to bring me another
when she went down to the market. I was afraid
of needing a cigarette one day and not being able
to find one. The women in the building usually
hung out at my place. They chatted and
constantly made coffee. I was no longer afraid of
Najla's presence as long as they were all around.
Rather, I could sense an invisible power taking
hold of me, allowing me to deflect the scorn and
sarcasm she directed at me. I wished death upon
her. I wished her ex-husband Abu Ali would
come back and take her away so I could live in
peace. The women of the building hung out at
my place. They opened the windows that I always
left shut, letting the sun in. I felt a light rush of
dizziness. The sunlight makes my eyes water, I
told Maha, who had pulled the curtains aside a
little. My eyes watered a lot when Josefa came out
of the kitchen carrying a tray of food from which
smoke curled upward and spread, warm and
appetizing, throughout the room. My heart
ignited once again when I heard Sara nearby.
"Eat, eat now!" Josefa told me in a familiar,
decisive tone. The photo albums that I opened
were always close by. I picked up the first one,
which began with a picture of me in the hospital
where I gave birth: I'm holding Sara in my arms,
looking at her; her eyes are closed. I had come to

Lebanon just weeks before she was born. The doctor examined me and said that it was still too early. My stomach was growing and my daughter was lengthening and widening in her little home. Not only was my stomach growing, but my entire body: my eyes, my nose, my mouth, and my ears. Every fiber of my being was pregnant with her. My fullness granted me an incomparable pleasure that lasted throughout my pregnancy, then dissipated and was gone a few weeks after she was born.

How beautiful I was when I walked through the hospital door. The nurse asked me to wait while they prepared the delivery room. Waves of pain both large and small crashed inside me: pains that surged and then broke, pains simultaneously tormenting and light. I thought I would surely die from only a few moments of such pain. It was as if my soul had been suspended somewhere between my womb and my neck and all it would take was a light push to pop it out like a hiccup. Pain penetrated deep inside me, into the labyrinth that stored all my desires, desires for death and desires for life. A wave crested. A long *Ahh* came out of my body but then was cut short. The nurse standing to my left put on her thick glasses. I looked at her. My clenched face shone under the harsh white light. "Hold out your arm, dear!" another one told me in a voice more commanding than my pain, who stood to my right and held a tube that connected the bag of clear fluid hanging above me to my artery that pumped pressurized red blood. I clenched my hand tightly around the metal edge of the bed. I waited for this wave—surging high toward the far reaches of my soul—to pass. "Straighten your arm, dear!" the second nurse bellowed in my face. "Please, I need some air... Wait... Just give me a few seconds..." I don't think she heard me. Instead, she just continued the conversation she was having with the other nurse. She was telling her about a friend of theirs who had lost her small dog the night before. It had been run over by a car. "The poor thing. If only it had been chained up properly, that never would have happened," said the one with glasses, as she propped up my feet after spreading my legs apart. She tied each foot to a cold metal stirrup with a broad leather strap.

My God, how did she ever come out? She just popped out into the world from inside me, as if she were riding on a toboggan, sledding on snow. This glittering and beautiful, tiny and sticky little girl slipped right out of me. Her eyes were wide open, amazed by the white world and the harsh light all around her. *Waaa... waaa*, she cried. The place was filled with her presence. I was empty.

Sara came out of me. My heart came out with her, as though my insides had been completely eviscerated: the kind of frightening emptiness that made me want to be filled with raw desire. When Rashad visited me in the hospital, I started telling him to fill me back up. I made room for him beside me on the narrow bed, begging him to fill me back up. I became like the base of a harvested wheat stalk, still fixed in the ground, calling out to the void, talking to my own barrenness. Fill me back up so that I might become whole again, a second time. "Crazy… you're crazy," he repeated, exasperated and harsh, pulling away from me. Then he left the room. I went home. Rashad went back to work in the Gulf. My headaches returned, sometimes to the point that my eyes glazed over and I could no longer see my daughter's face. I was stricken with dizzy spells. My mother carried Sara in her arms, softly singing her to sleep. I fell asleep, too.

I returned to the Gulf, where the year only has two seasons. How I love the seasons. I returned bearing clothes, toys, food, and suitcases filled with everything the little girl I carried in my arms might need.

The telephone rang. I lifted the receiver. "Hello? Hello?" Nobody there. I said hello a second time. Nobody answered. But I could hear someone breathing, someone standing somewhere holding the receiver, holding still. Was it the one who kidnapped my daughter? He wanted her to talk to me but then changed his mind. "Hello... this is Warda... put Sara on... I'm her mother." Continuous beeping echoed in my ears. The line was dead.

Josefa sat beside me on the edge of the bed, holding a bowl of hot soup in her hand. She filled the spoon, raised it toward her lips and blew on it again and again. She brought it close to my mouth, which was dry and slightly ajar, and fed me.

My cousin, who married a Cypriot woman and lived on the island, used to visit me. He brought money from my husband and a letter sent to an address in Limasol from Sara that said she had arrived in America. I looked at the letter and saw that the mail had delivered it all the way from America. Sara was in America! I heard myself say it, but how could that be? My cousin wouldn't show me any of the letters he received from Rashad, but I understood that he wasn't thinking of ever bringing me to America. He had submitted his citizenship application; he'll stay there with Sara. How long had it been since my husband left the Gulf? I asked my cousin, who told me that my family had left the Gulf just after I returned to Lebanon and that Rashad was moving all his work to America as well.

I remember how, just before the last time I came back to Lebanon, Rashad asked me to go back first, saying that he would get Sara an entry visa and then send for her. "An entry visa?" I asked him confusedly. "But she's my daughter," I said. "She'll enter my country with me, where my house and my family are, with me." "But she isn't Lebanese and she can't be," Rashad replied. The next day I went to the embassy. I was certain that Rashad was making the whole thing up. I told the embassy employee that she was my daughter, my own flesh and blood. I told him everything, showed him my passport and my daughter's papers to prove that I was her mother. But he refused and insisted that I submit an entry visa application. He said things that were a lot like what Rashad had said. The application would take a while to get approved. I didn't understand. The matter seemed impossible to me. "You go first!" my husband told me. I came to Beirut and, instead of sending Sara to me later, he took her with him and traveled to America, a far-off place. How could I get there?

I accompanied my cousin to Cyprus, where he lived in a city overlooking blue like the blue of Beirut. I could get a tourist visa there that would take me to Sara. I rushed to present my documents. No doubt they'd give me an entry visa when they saw my hair that Josefa had dyed blonde for me.

In Limasol, I waited every day for a call from the embassy. My cousin's Cypriot wife wouldn't speak to me. She came out of her room and began shouting at my cousin in her own language. I didn't understand a thing. He told her to calm down. Sometimes he spoke Arabic and cursed the hour that woman entered his house. Which woman? No doubt he was referring to me. It didn't matter. His wife left for work. He left, too. He worked with Lebanese people. He bought plane tickets for them that were cheaper than what the travel agencies charged. He also guaranteed them the necessary documentation to get entry visas. I rotated the telephone dial. From there I could call anywhere in the world. My brother's wife picked up. "Put my brother on," I said. My brother answered. "Don't call at this hour," he said. Why was he like that, why couldn't he handle hearing the sound of my voice. "When should I call?" He always told me not to call now! I called him dozens of times, at home and in the office. I asked him for Rashad's phone number. I called Rashad and then sat down to wait for the visa that he promised me. I've been waiting here for three months.

In the last few days, my cousin's wife hasn't been able to stand me any longer. She said that she spent her entire salary on the bill for the phone calls I had been making every day. She said I bothered the neighbors while they were sleeping, that I puttered around with metal things in the kitchen at night, making a ruckus that woke everyone up. She said everything without saying much of anything. She didn't say that I couldn't sleep, that my eyes were red and swollen, that a terrible pain was digging into my eyeball like the pecking of a ferocious bird. She didn't say that I no longer saw very much at all, or that the curtains in my room remained drawn all day, or that the woman who looked out the window of the opposite building used to peer in on me and call out to my brother's wife— Dimitra, *agapi mou*—to invite her over for coffee. How gargantuan and fat she was. Just the thought of her shape had me drowning in laughter. No doubt I had laughed in front of other people at times. I only realized that when people stood around staring at me. Then I would look down to stare at myself, at my body and my clothes, to ask myself what they were all staring at.

I wait for a call from the embassy. They want a sponsorship letter from Rashad that he still hasn't sent. I wait but don't have the patience to wait any longer. I run through the wide streets, the streets that are always lit up. There are no cars on the road. I let the rain soak my head. When cars pass by, their tires slide on the rain that slicks down the street. I keep on running. I cross over to the other side of the street. Raindrops sluice across my face, streaming down my chin to my neck. I smile. I reach the opposite sidewalk: the coast with the Cinchona trees and the wide sandy beach. I walk among the trees. My feet sink into the sand. I press down harder and run along the length of the beach, the crashing waves pack the sand together, soaking it. The waves crash and recede. I submerge my feet in the salty water. I keep running. I follow the wave as it recedes. It plays with me, inviting me, opening its arms to me. I keep running: from Beirut, to the Gulf, to America: I keep running. Ropes pull the sky toward the earth. I feel the pull of the ropes on my body. The rain intensifies and reaches my bones. The rain soaks through my hair until I can't see anything at all. The water is lukewarm; the autumn wind hasn't chilled it yet. I plunge in deeper, to where the wave disappears. The water surges. I plunge into the deep, to where the water is warmer, lovelier than the streets illuminated by dull yellow lamps. The moon shines wide and full above me. I see my own shadow chasing after me. I press on. Why does the sea now seem like a desert in the heart of the night? A desert like the one Rashad took me to. I run further, fleeing the desert, but exhaustion weighs on my head and shoulders, like someone urging me on toward the deep.

In the distance, there are shimmering lights, the lights of boats passing into the heart of the sea and flickering out. I see Sara beckoning me. My body sags. It becomes fresh and light. It can walk on water. My body moves toward Sara. Her hand is still raised, waving in the air. Part of my body is tugged forward as though I'm not walking, as though I'm rising and falling, like a child's car in an amusement park spun in circles and then hoisted into the atmosphere. I rise until I nearly touch the sky, then quickly sink again. My hand rises, waving. My body softens; my balled hands relax. Bubbles emerge like voices from the depths of the sea. In the womb of the water: seaweed and sunken treasures. Everything is submerged and then vanishes.

Camilia

I used to think about flying a lot. I would imagine that I could fly without wings. I would become as light as a feather and touch down in distant lands, arriving there before I had ever actually seen the place. Sometimes I would step on the treetops, taking care not to break them.

I used to think about flying whenever I went out with Pierre and sat behind him on his motorcycle. I would hold onto him tightly as the speed of the motorcycle tried to outdo the flying that began in my body's round places, from my bellybutton and somewhere deep inside my head: flying across exhilarating limitless distances. The metal helmet I wore to protect my head and that covered my eyes and part of my face didn't prevent me from rattling on and on about passionate

dreams I had. *Hold on tight!* Pierre would say when
we leaned into a sharp slope on the road outside
town. He would rev the throttle hard and we'd fly
high above the earth. Fresh air stung my face and
the scents of trees thrusting into the sky became
stronger. My heart flew and then suddenly
plummeted in awe as my body burned and my
face flushed in the pleasurable heat.

Pierre was unlike me in every way, but that didn't
bother me. When he looked at me, I could sense
an intimacy that was padded by silence.
Sometimes small talk broke up our silence. We
didn't need to say anything, though; when I was
with him, I didn't feel like I had to say anything.
Vast spaces opened up before us: we had no idea
where we were headed, so I just wrapped my arms
around his body and threw my face against the
shoulder of his leather jacket, taking pleasure in
its cold, sharp smell.

I can still smell it, even now. News of the war
reached us from distant locations—at least that's
what I thought. We weren't afraid of the clouds of
smoke rising from the concrete wilderness when
we saw them from afar. It was as if we lived on an
island in the middle of a sea filled with killer
whales. We never once wanted to go down to the
water, but the sea brought its dangers to us
anyway. I wasn't afraid until the night Pierre was

killed. That's when I first became afraid of the
war. I began to fear the panic I saw in my own
eyes and in the eyes of the people all around me.
At first, the idea that the war was on its way
somehow didn't seem so bad. It had entered our
houses by way of the news visitors brought with
them or through the radio and TV. That's how it
got in. I was affected when I saw a powerful and
surprising transformation in our daily affairs, in
our way of life. Schools closed, opened, then
closed again. My aunt Shams no longer told me
to go to bed early; my grandmother stopped
scolding me when I came home late. I could leave
the house without anyone asking me anything.
The field hospital, the media, Party meetings and
a whole lot more: the geography of the entire
place had expanded. We began to own the place.
We used to be only visitors. It was easy for me to
adapt to this new life, easier than adapting to the
orderly life most girls in town were used to.
Maybe that was because I grew up in a house
with no men. No one exercised absolute control
over my decisions. The only man who ever came
into our house was my maternal uncle. When he
married a Muslim woman from Jordan and
moved there, his visits became less frequent. Ever
since I was a little girl, I had been certain of the
fact that I was never going to turn out like my
aunt Shams, that I would never throw my life
away in some windowless kitchen. At first, I

would get angry when she called me insolent or said that I was loose and didn't deserve any respect from her or from my grandmother. But after a few years, her description of me became a source of pride, certifying that I would never turn out like her.

When I was first getting to know him, Pierre would kiss me on the cheek whenever he came over. I was thrilled by that novel tradition, which was totally foreign to us except among relatives and immediate family. He would approach my aunt, extend his hand to her and move in for a kiss. My aunt would reach out her hand and kiss him bashfully, muttering something about how he was like a younger brother to her. But when Pierre wanted to greet my grandmother, she responded while keeping her distance. She would stiffen up a little, as though getting ready for a fight, and then she covered her head well and hid her hands under a broad white *mandeel*. My aunt would kiss him and ask about his mother, his grandmother, and his sister, who she used to see everyday as she walked to the town's main street to wait for a taxi to take her to Beirut, where she taught French. She asked him about everyone. After he had left, she slammed the door behind him. She came into my room and glared at me, "What does that Christian want from us after all this? Do you want the shaykh to forbid your grandmother from going to the *majlis* and to say that she lives under the same roof with an infidel? Do you want everyone to say that I did a poor job raising you? What was he doing in your room anyway?" "We were just studying, Auntie, we were just studying," I answered, exasperated. "Studying how to thresh the harvest in the field this year will break your bones, *inshallah*," my aunt intoned. I got up from my chair with visible indignation and went to slam the door in her face. Just then, my aunt took off her shoes and flipped them over so that the heel was facing upward, saying furiously, "I hope he doesn't come back, I hope he doesn't know the way back to our house."

Pierre became friends with my neighbor Akram and we all started studying together. Our late nights lasted until sunrise. His interest in me satisfied my own self-conceit. When he visited me for the first time, I busied myself preparing fruit salad. He followed me into the kitchen to peel oranges and wash grapes for me. I didn't ask him to help, but it thrilled me when he did. He sat down to keep me company as I cleared the table. When I refused his invitation to the movies, he kissed a lock of my hair to say goodbye. "You'll regret the times you refused my invitation." He was right.

We started out meeting on the road leading to the town graveyards. First we passed by the

Druze graves that fanned out across the low foothills, nestled among the oak trees. Their walls were built out of jutting gray stone and their small doors were painted black. At the end of the foothills, toward the west, there was a short path that led down to the valley where the winter rains collected. The Christian graves were built on a small hill overlooking that road. There was a small forest of fir and poplar trees separating the two sects' cemeteries. The story of our rendezvous began one day years back, when my grandmother told me of a large oak tree, said to be hundreds of years old and inhabited by a black serpent. It was believed to feed on corpses, gouging out their eyes and eating their entrails. Once it was sated, it would return to its lair in the heart of the oak tree. It never came out to the road and no one ever saw it. It was said that there was a secret tunnel connecting its lair to the graves and that it would never harm anyone or dare cross a road used by the living. I went down into the valley and searched for the largest, thickest oak trees. I hoped to catch a glimpse of the serpent even as the beating of my heart grew louder. There were gigantic boulders under one large tree, ruins of a Roman cemetery. I met Pierre for the first time there by chance. He was alone, crouching in a tree not far from the oak. As soon as I arrived, he started pelting me with strange fruit and making wheezing sounds to frighten me. I didn't look up

and I didn't move, because I had seen him just
before I walked under the tree. My detachment
and lack of interest turned him on. He scrambled
down as swiftly as a cheetah and stood in front of
me. Then he thrust his hand inside his bulging
pocket and pulled out a handful of red hawthorn
fruit. "They're the tastiest fruit," he said, handing
me one. I'd never seen such fruit before. That tree,
too, I hadn't noticed before, and it also amazed
me. I knew that this was his secret hiding place
and that he came here every day. His hiding place
became ours for years to come.

My rendezvous with Pierre started distracting
me from the war, which had moved in closer.
When we went down to the beach together, I said
how I wanted to run away. He said that we could
run off together. He stood up, shook the sand off
his body and started to walk. I walked next to
him. He rented a raft and I lay down in it. He
started rowing slowly and rhythmically. I lifted
my head and watched the shoreline recede. The
sounds thinned out and the crashing of the waves
grew louder, filling every cell in my head. I
studied his body, young and muscular, as the sun
tanned it and the hairs on his chest turned
golden. The sun coated my body and part of my
face. I saw his calm eyes watching over me as I
fell asleep. I felt as though I were slipsliding on
wet clouds; I fell without getting hurt. I started to
dance and the clouds turned into trees; I started

to move my feet more slowly. I saw a bird and
tried to catch it. As soon as I imagined I had it in
my hands, I saw it fly away suddenly, soaring into
the sky. I raised my eyes to see it but a powerful
glare blinded me and set my face ablaze. I felt
then as though a shadow had descended and
begun to spread all over my body like a cloud.
Soft moisture warmed me, spread over me,
protected me from the glare of the sun. My
forehead and my eyes were still exposed to the
heat. I kept my eyes closed. It was a warm
wetness and my body was meeting the glare from
the sky with a glare of its own, a glare flickering
from the depths of my soul, igniting me. The
horizon was wide, spreading out to infinity. The
sea was choppy and a layer of warm, salty
moisture covered the raft. Water splashed us,
cooling us as the raft rocked and rolled under our
bodies. I slept, and when I woke, the sun was
high. Pierre lay next to me. I reached out and
caressed his face, and closed my eyes once again.
Bliss enveloped us. There was no need for words.
"Where do you want to go?" he asked me, picking
the oar up again. I was disturbed at the thought
that our relationship might not have been going
anywhere. Still, an inchoate desire spurred me to
see it through, a desire that filled my soul and left
no room for anxiety.

Akram had become my superior in our cell of
the Party and I had started calling him Comrade

Jaafar. He inquired about my relationship with Pierre. I said that he was a good friend, but that we had no real intentions beyond that. I could see a repressed desire for me in Akram's eyes, which he concealed hurriedly by talking about some book he was carrying, something boring, and I knew once he got started it would never end. He went on talking as I started reminiscing about all the nice memories we shared from when we were little, and smiled. Akram noticed then that I was distracted, that I wasn't listening to what he was saying. I told him how I was just remembering him in his wet clothes and his shouting that time I'd poured a jug of water all on him; there were small frogs swimming in there that we had captured together from the pond. Akram didn't even smile and in his annoyance asked me to forget I had ever known him and to only call him by his Party pseudonym. He also told me to introduce myself by the Party name he had chosen for me at one of our meetings. Those meetings always seemed like a kind of game I was playing with Akram. I performed on this stage, and after the grand finale returned home, to the real world.

Summer was coming to an end and we started preparing for the celebration that happened at the end of every summer. All the town club members were busy making the *kermis* festival a success, maybe because of unspoken concerns that it would be incomplete somehow. I was supposed to sell tickets for the event with the help of Pierre and his motorcycle, but I couldn't find him. I looked for him at the club, at his house, and at Akram's. I waited for him. I waited a long time. But he didn't come that night. His absence was the harbinger of the war's arrival in our town. The war came. It awoke from its slumber. It awoke and took off its mask, the mask that always hung over our conversations, our language, and our daily affairs, the mask of *how humane the Other is and how we love him so, the Other who is of us and in us and whom we cannot live without.*

Things in town had changed; it was no longer the same place: something I could feel but not see all around us as the sun rose. When the sun had set, it left behind creatures trying to get used to a new language, exhumed from their bottomless past, a language that buried in its letters and behind its words a fear that was still alive. The sun dipped slowly behind the sea and fear mixed with the remaining daylight, which too slipped away, never to return. Darkness shrouded us in madness and we accepted it like a man resigned to drowning. Gossip spun around and around in the morning and didn't stop at night. I heard it, Akram heard it, Nadim heard it, too. It rolled down from the top of the mountain where Pierre had been found murdered. It rolled down to our houses. We washed our faces and carried on the same conversation. We ate but carried on the same conversation. We went to the bathroom. We looked at ourselves in the mirror but carried on the same conversation. One day passed; another arrived. The same conversation tortured us. It's either madness or conversation—there's no other choice.

Pierre was a member of the Party, the Phalange Party. That's how rumors spread. Pierre has been murdered! He, not me; he, not Nadim, not Akram. Us, not them. He had been murdered, not me. I found that I had a different name. A name takes on the shape of a person, transformed into either victimizer or victim. What happened might have comforted some of us, but that comfort was only a passing illusion.

Nadim moved away. When he came to say goodbye, he said, "I can't stay silent here and I don't want to go insane either." He packed up all his stuff and left. What would I do, staying in this place?

I remember the coming of winter when I was a little girl. The snow fell thick and the schools were closed. We would go outside to play in the snow all day. The sun smiled down at us, making our cheeks and noses ruddy. We might make a snowman—short, funny looking, white. When its head fell off and rolled down the winding road that led to our house, we chased it as the sun chased us. Then the sun rose higher and our shadows stretched between the snowball and us. The head grew larger and its color changed and we weren't able to carry it back, return it to where it had been. It became larger than we were. We disappeared and our shadow disappeared. I don't remember if it ever snowed again after that. We haven't seen snow since that year; we never made another snowman.

A week went by and I couldn't go to school. At the beginning of the following week, I went back to school, and back to deluding myself that nothing had happened. In history class, I said, "I need to go outside." Dizziness overwhelmed me, I shivered from a high fever. I looked at the sky through the window of the car that drove me home, as words shrieked through my head, tormenting me. My grandmother had heard that Pierre was a Phalangist and my uncle said so, too. When I cried, my aunt went off, telling me what a whore I was. "That's it, enough," she said. "I'm sending you to your mother's. To hell with you. I can't be responsible for you anymore." My aunt went into a panic over my constant crying and the town midwife was summoned to examine me. I was sweating from the fever; it was burning me up inside. "In the name of God most gracious, most merciful," my grandmother said. "To ward off the evil eye," my aunt said as she melted three bullets in a metal pot over the fire. I watched my grandmother pick up the pot and look inside. My aunt fetched rosewater and gave me some to drink. I tried to spit it out but she cupped her hand over my mouth and with her other hand clamped my nostrils shut. I closed my eyes and saw the eyes of many people who seemed familiar, but when they came a little closer, I discovered I didn't know them after all. I turned around and tried to get away from them but they were faster than me and grabbed me. They tied me up and put me to bed. The woman holding the pot wasn't my grandmother: She was my mother. I still have a picture of her from her wedding day in which she wore a white dress and held a bouquet of silk flowers. I asked my aunt what color the flowers were that my mother held in that black-and-white photo. I imagined the colors of those flowers, smelled their fragrance, touched them.

My fever got worse and I watched my aunt Shams pull me by the hand through the churchyard to take me home, shouting, "Don't look at the cross in church or you'll go blind." She asked me not to talk to the priest on Sunday when he came to our house. She berated me: Christ is for us and not for them. My grandmother yanked me by the ear when I started to make the vow, "My hand on the cross, I'm not lying." I had learned that from Leila, who went to the missionary school. The midwife took a talisman, stuck it through my wet cotton shirt and poked a hole in the shirt with a metal safety pin. The pin punctured my skin. It hurt but no blood came out. I didn't scream, but I did hear myself say that I had seen him, that I had seen Pierre scrawling the symbol of the Phalange Party on the wall of his house; he also wore it on his clothes. On several occasions, I had bumped into him as he was coming furtively into town, as agile as a thief. Pierre was different. He had to be.

They pulled my head back, bound my hands. No, I mean, Pierre's hands. I saw myself lying in my bed. My bed was wet, my body was warm and sweat dampened my hair and my back. My mother sat near my head, placed a washcloth soaked with water and vinegar on my forehead and my stomach. She rested her hand there briefly, and then replaced the piece of cloth with another she'd preheated. I tried to speak but she didn't hear me. The words got stuck in my throat. My lips moved. I closed my eyes, then opened them again. I remembered that I didn't know what my mother's face looked like because she left the country when I was only ten months old and never came back. Several years later, she gave birth to another daughter named Camilia. The woman holding my hand and raising the clumps of wet hair from my forehead and face was my grandmother, Hamida. I blacked out again, into the labyrinth of dizziness and fever, and saw myself lying on a bed covered with white satin sheets. There were flowers placed all around me and I choked on their smell. I grabbed at my neck and my aunt had to pull my hand away. Faces and eyes surrounded me: Pierre's sister, his aunt, his mother, and his grandmother all cried in silence. Then they said that I was dead. I tried to sit up but I couldn't. I murmured that I was still alive, that I didn't kill Pierre. I repeated several times that I didn't kill him. But they didn't believe me. They shoved my body down on the bed again and pushed my head against the sheet. Then a woman stepped forward with a thin scarf across her face and two red pearls hanging from her ears. Is there such a thing as a red pearl? I asked. But she didn't answer; she just squeezed my hand. I looked at her face and I couldn't tell if she was a man or a woman. Her lips were as thin as a young girl's and her hands were rough like those of a laborer. I held onto the side of the bed and tried to sit up but she pushed me back down and tucked the cover over me. My senses drifted and darkness and silence settled over me.

We can't guarantee protection for anyone, Comrade Jaafar said. I returned home on foot at sundown. I left the bustling Party headquarters, which was on the hill among the pine and cypress trees. When I was a little girl, the center was a beautiful school, an English school belonging to the Protestant mission. During the war, it had been converted into Party headquarters and a meeting place for young men from town who were members of numerous parties. The garage was converted into an artillery storehouse. In one room of the spacious school, a field hospital was set up to tend to the wounded. This room directly faced the towns that the assault came from, but none of us ever thought of emptying it. We can't guarantee protection for anyone, not even ourselves. In the distance between the headquarters and my house, I asked myself when it would be my turn. I asked myself and I was afraid. The raindrops started soaking my hair so I hurried even more quickly toward home.

My body quivered like a leaf stripped from its tree. My limbs quaked like fragments of a corpse as I slipped under the covers in my room. I could hear my aunt's and my grandmother's irregular breathing. The two of them slept in one room and left the other rooms empty. The beds there were always made, the sheets clean. I was woken up by the sound of pebbles and dirt crashing into the house and spreading across the floor during the shelling. In the beginning, I used to pull the blanket up over my face, hide my head completely. I believed that nothing could hurt me as long as my face was under the covers. My aunt would get up and wake my grandmother. Together, they would hurry down to the ground floor, calling for me to join them. There we would recover the sense of security that we never truly lost.

There was a woman from Metn province, Therese, who had shown up with her husband during the first phase of the war, after her entire family had been murdered right in front of her. She came to town and rented the ground floor of our house. The ground floor was beautiful when she partitioned the *qabu* into a salon and a dining room. She also painted the large iron door a beautiful shade of pink. Therese would open the door every morning and look out onto the small garden: its neglected ancient walnut tree, some apricot and loquat trees. Whenever the shelling began, Therese would open the door and look up toward our large balcony, shouting at us to get our things together and take off, that the Phalangist convoy had arrived: "Hurry up, get out of here!" When we first met her, we used to listen, to hurry without thinking, searching as fast as we could for our most prized possessions, throwing them in a suitcase, getting the hell out of there. Each one of us headed in a different direction. But as we gathered our things, gathered all our possessions, my grandmother would sit on the edge of the bed watching us. And we never ended up closing the suitcases, not even once, and we never left.

When I heard Therese calling me in that frightened, scratchy voice, I would look down at her over the edge of the balcony. The lines in her face grew deeper in moments of fear, terrifying me. Her pupils would dilate and grow blacker. She looked like a scared cat. For a long time, Therese persisted in thinking that the militias were following her. I would smile at her and nod, saying, "Don't worry, nothing's going to happen." Then I would go back inside.

The ground floor was cozy: a large room where people lived and slept, sheltered from outside by an adjoining room, which was connected to a high *qabu* with two windows near the ceiling. We weren't afraid to sit in that *qabu*. My grandmother always said that nothing, not even a bomb, could destroy what my grandfather had built. Sometimes we would sleep in there with the many neighbors who came over seeking shelter. When they arrived, I would get up and move someplace else. Over time, I stopped being surprised when I woke in the middle of the night and saw the faces of several people sleeping beside me. I got used to it, to my aunt waking up early to go outside with Therese to make sure there was enough food and water for everyone. When my aunt came back, she would start burning some firewood in the backyard to make loaf after loaf of bread. My grandmother didn't stay with us most nights, going instead with some other elderly people to the *majlis* where they prayed and read from the *kitab al-hikma* for hours on end.

I went home. No sooner did I arrive than I left again. I moved back and forth like a bouncing ball creating a sound that prevailed over its movement. I thought about Nadim for a moment. I wanted to see him but then I remembered that he wasn't around anymore, that he had moved abroad. I retraced my steps and headed toward Samer's house, the young man who had recently come to town from Ayn al-Rummaneh. He told me about a girl he'd left behind there. He told me jokes and made me laugh. My friend Leila got married and moved to London. I went back to my grandmother's house when it started getting dark. I went back only to leave again right away. I saw my grandmother letting down her hair. Since my childhood, her curls had always been the same length. They reached past her waist, all the way to the small of her back. Does hair stop growing with age or did it just seem that way because her hair was so thick and curly? I would leave the house whenever it seemed like people were coming back to sit or get ready for bed. That's when I would leave. I would find waiting for me one of the guys who had come to live in town but whose name I couldn't recall.

What's the point in learning people's names anyhow?

A letter arrived from my mother, saying that her factory was coming along well. Who cares about your factory, mom? My aunt opened the letters. She knew that I no longer opened them if she left them on the table in the entryway. I just looked at the beautiful postage stamps affixed to them and asked my aunt to save them because I loved to collect stamps. Then I left again. I'm not going to open that woman's letters. Why should I?

I've never settled down in one place and I'm not going to. I press on, toward the unknown. I immerse myself in the outside world, let my soul fill with its hours and its details. I allow the smells of the outside to penetrate the pores of my body and my memory. The outside becomes a part of me and I become a part of it. But I quickly get bored as my soul yearns for more. I came back, then went out again. I didn't come home until dawn. "You wicked stray girl." I heard these garbled words coming out of my grandmother's mouth. She had taken out her dentures and placed them in a glass of salt water on the nightstand. My aunt opened her eyes, raised her head from the pillow in exaggerated sluggishness. "Where have you been until the break of dawn?" she asked me, fuming. Her voice came out deep and wet with her chronic cough. I ground my teeth—the two bitches! I'd taken off my shoes before I came in and didn't turn the light on. So how did they see me come in? I switched the light on with an exaggerated click. I turned on all the lights in the house. I went into the kitchen and opened all the cupboards. I took out plates I didn't need. I opened the refrigerator and took out all of the food. I didn't eat anything, just drank a glass of water. I left everything in chaos. I went into my room, threw myself down on the bed and immediately fell asleep.

I saw new boys in town. Families that constantly wanted to prove that they belonged. There were more and more families telling more and more tragic stories of the places they'd left behind. They believed it would be easier for them to fit in here if they went on about the humiliation they'd been subjected to. Not one of them ever said anything about being happy where they used to live. They extracted small events of their pasts from their memory and mulled them over repeatedly to prove that their displacement was more than a spur-of-the-moment occurrence. Not one of them ever said a single nice thing about the people they'd left, the people who'd forced them to leave.

The young people among the new arrivals had fled the coastal regions, the city and its suburbs. They spoke various dialects. They combed their hair in a style that the boys of the town weren't used to. Music blared from their cars when they cruised the narrow streets. The music got mixed up with the roar of the engines; it sounded broken and violent. I started seeing some of them at Party meetings, meetings that seemed interesting enough at first. I told myself that the meetings were fun because I met a lot of boys there, but boredom quickly overtook me. I began to meet the boys outside. It was more fun that way. And it was fun to cruise around neighboring towns all night. Samer would drive his father's car and another guy would follow us in a military jeep that he had borrowed from his brother, who was in a militia. The jeep was packed with young men. We honked the horns freely and let screams from deep inside our chests echo in the darkness of the roads and among the houses. We could hear the sounds of those who our screaming had woken up. Our excitement peaked, our laughter and cursing grew louder, followed by gunfire as one of us shot into the air. Sometimes the night's silence was pregnant with possibility, sometimes it frightened us. After he had given me the wheel, I asked Samer, sitting beside me, why we didn't turn off the streetlights? Why were they lit at such a late hour anyway? "Hit the streetlights, switch them off. Come on, break a streetlight or break the window of that store," I kept on saying. Then I pointed at the target. Samer picked up the machine gun resting on the seat behind me, squeezed his finger on the trigger and a continuous burst of fire shot out of the barrel, which he balanced on the edge of the car window. He missed the streetlight but that didn't stop him from trying again. I stomped down on the accelerator and the car zoomed off, peeling out as the passengers behind us screamed louder, piercing the void.

I didn't understand the conversations that went on during the meetings at headquarters. When Akram asked me to throw out my gum, I turned my back on him and blew bubbles, snapping them loudly, like a clap of thunder. He would give me a book and tell me to read it so that we could discuss it at his place one week later. He gave me books but I didn't read them because they were boring and didn't say anything about real people. I had always loved reading stories about people. When I sat down in front of him in that small living room, he was holding a book and asked me to move. The electricity cut out for a few minutes and he got up to fetch a candle. I got up with him but I don't quite know how our bodies found each other, made contact. His body was close to mine for a few moments and then he started pressing his weight down against my chest. When the electricity came back on, his damp, red face made me laugh. How strong I seemed in that moment. I seemed stronger than him, than his big talk, than all the books that fell out of his hand and onto the ground.

Not a single man lived in our house. I was born and raised and grew up, and not a single man lived in our house. "It's hard for a household to carry on without a man around," my grandmother used to say, and still stay as bright as my aunt's sheets on the laundry line. "If your father were here, I wouldn't have this burden of raising a girl all by myself," my aunt added. His absence didn't bother me; I felt an extreme, boundless freedom, a freedom that was apparent in my eyes and my behavior. Whenever I talked to my girlfriends about it, I could read in their eyes how much they longed for the sudden death of their own fathers. I secretly enjoyed it, but also concealed jealousy that gnawed at me from inside whenever I saw mothers coming to school in the afternoon with lunch for their daughters.

"I'm sending you to your father's. To hell with you," my aunt said in the night, grabbing me by the hand and shoving me inside the house. After my father died in a car accident in Argentina, my aunt stopped saying such things. After his death, my mother married their partner in the spinning factory and then had another child. She rushed to have another child. She gave birth to a girl who she named Camilia—that is, she gave her my name. She said that she missed me. Is that why she gave my name to her other daughter? Did she miss me that much? I would ask, as the anger grew inside me like a tumor. I really was furious: at my father, at my mother, at all the women around me, at the war that my mother used as a pretense not to come back. Why didn't the two of them take me with them? I asked the same question over and over. My mother kept on writing that she was going to come back at the beginning of the summer. Every letter ended with a sentence that I had memorized. "I'll see you this summer *inshallah*." But she kept on delaying her return from one summer to the next. Meanwhile I grew up and my mother got closer to old age. When my aunt got upset with me, she would remind me how she had begged my mother to take me with her and how my father had refused, claiming that she was going to be working, just like him, and that the two of them didn't know anyone there to entrust with a breastfeeding child. They were moving away to make some money. My grandmother cried and said that our land can't hold onto its children, while my aunt started to beat her breast, claiming that I was the reason she still wasn't married.

My uncle was the only man who ever visited us and stayed over at our house. One day, through my classroom window, I saw him get out of a taxi in the town square and head down the road that slopes to our house carrying thin, dark paper bags. I slipped out during the last hour of class, while the teacher had his face to the blackboard explaining the Arabic lesson in a muted voice. Our teacher, Daoud, immersed himself in his explanations like someone talking to himself while we sat still, staring at him, monitoring the lethargic movements of his body in front of the blackboard, chalk dust flying all around him. We made paper airplanes out of the handouts he gave us and threw them at one another. They flew high into the air, as light as moths, not making a sound. The day before my uncle arrived, some girls from my class dared me to come to school barefoot. When the next day I did, winning the bet, they sat in a circle around me and squawked in amazement. My uncle looked down at my small, blackened feet and asked me angrily if I showed up to school like that every day, if I had any shoes at all. I tried explaining to him about the class dare, but he just handed me the bags of candy and motioned to tell me that there was no use in trying to explain, urging me ahead of him toward home. I walked slowly because I wanted to see the look on his face. I thought, I want to see how men look when they get angry. Do they get angry like my aunt and beat their chests, scream and wail? I didn't want to turn around so I started bringing my steps closer together, shortening them and slowing my pace, staring at the ground

so he would think I was just making sure I didn't
step on pebbles and thorns in my bare feet. When
we arrived at home, there was nobody there. My
aunt was out in the field. I quickly put some shoes
on and went to escort my grandmother home
from the *majlis*. My uncle had letters from my
mother; she had also sent pictures and money.

The entrance to the *majlis* was lit dimly.
Lights flickered in lanterns spread out on the
ground all around those praying. Inside was a large
salon with a wooden ceiling, divided into two
areas by a white curtain. The curtain was held up
on one side by nails hammered into the wall and
was left hanging open slightly so people could pass
through to the other side. The salon looked onto
the outer room, which was for men, but the inner
room behind the curtain was reserved for women.
If a woman wanted to go outside before the men
were finished, she had to be sure that her head and
face were completely covered except for one eye.
She would have to cover her hands and the upper
part of her body with a long white muslin *mandeel*,
which she also wrapped around her head. I stood
there confused, forgetting why I had come in the
first place. I stood there staring at the bearded old
men sitting in a circle. In front of some of them
there were religious books on low tables, opened
to pages with words scrawled on them in
longhand. They were reading. I stood there
listening to the slow rhythm of their voices. Their

voices were deep, as though they were coming
from some distant place. Their voices sounded as
though they had just finished a high, long cry:
pure and crystal clear. When one of them noticed
me, he stopped reading. He averted his gaze and
twice asked for almighty God's forgiveness. May
God disgrace the devil, said another. A terrifying
silence prevailed in the room, followed by a similar
silence in the women's room. A woman peeked
her covered head through the curtain and scolded
me, telling me I had to leave because my clothes
were inappropriate in that place. I took off
running scared toward home.

The outer front of the *majlis* never looked the
same after the bombing. Its polished yellow stone
walls were destroyed and huge concrete walls
with small, narrow windows were erected in their
place. The guard of the *majlis* came from the Jabal
Druze with his wife and two kids. He tended the
land surrounding it and his wife cleaned the
inside every day. When the fighting got really
bad, he and his large family went back to Syria
and the townspeople never saw him again.

When my uncle sat down to dinner with us,
my aunt served him first, saying that he looked
weak and yellow-faced. When he left the table to
wash his hands, my aunt mumbled that his yellow
face was from living in the city and sleeping with

loose women. My paternal aunt was older than my maternal uncle by a few years, but her cheeks flushed whenever she was near him, betraying what she'd been trying to hide and what I could discern ever since I started understanding something about men and women.

My uncle was still a university student and rarely came to visit us in the mountains. He used to study, eat, and sleep in the same place. Once, he told me about his room, which overlooked trees that bloomed with colorful flowers but never bore fruit. He told me about the vast blue sea that spread out before him, where he went swimming with his friends every day. The hours I spent with my uncle gave me pleasure even though he would have preferred to be alone reading. My uncle would sit in the small room on the couch opposite me and stretch out his long legs until his feet touched the edge of the metal bed. I would ask him all about my mother: her shape, her color, her eyes, about any birthmarks she might have had, if he could recall. Still staring at the book in his hands, he would answer as though he was talking about a woman he had no connection to; he wasn't passionate when he spoke about her. And when I asked him if I looked like her at all, he said that we were alike in our stubbornness, recalling how he had asked me on several occasions to stop getting my hair cut like a boy, but to no avail.

"Take me with you to Beirut," I said to him. But he repeated that there was nowhere for me to sleep, that they didn't allow the mixing of the sexes in the university where he lived, even if the girl was his niece. My aunt refused to set foot in that room as long as my uncle was staying there. During his several-day visits, she didn't go in to straighten the room up or make the bed or dust. She left his room as it was for as long he stayed with us. When he returned to the city, she went in, opened up all the windows and took the sheets and blankets off the bed. Then she piled them on the floor near the door to be taken and washed. She picked up the cotton mattress, took it off the bed and dragged it outside into the blazing sun, which was bright enough to raise the dead, as she always said. She started cleaning the couch, the table, and the sides of the bed with a disinfectant solution mixed with water, claiming that the room reeked with the man's odor. Her small eyes flashed when she said that the smell could only be eliminated with disinfectants. When my uncle got married, my aunt made a beautiful blanket for his wife. When he brought his Jordanian wife to our house for the first time, my aunt let them sleep in my parents' room, which no one went in, the room with the large wooden bed in the middle.

"Take me with you to Beirut," I always said to Dr. Muhammad, who worked shifts at the town field hospital where I worked. He came three days a week to treat the wounded and teach us how to give injections and how to tend to the sick. "Where would you like to go?" he asked me flirtingly, touching my face with his fingertips. Then I took take the plates of food for the wounded to the kitchen. The doctor followed me. "I want to go anywhere I can," I told him. "You're luck, my little one, is to be a girl here, among the smells of drugs and rancid blood wafting from the patients' beds." He added, "I can't do anything for you." Growing more desperate, I said, "I want the school year to be over already. School's closed here anyway. I don't want anything more than for you to take me with you to Beirut."

"Take me with you to Beirut!" I said to the doctor, who occasionally spent the night in the hospital if there was an emergency. Nawal the nurse brought piping-hot cups of tea. She sat on an empty bed and stretched out, complaining about the pain in her legs. Thin white curtains separated our beds. "Where would you like me to take you?" Muhammad asked me. "There's nothing worth moving for. Sleep, get some sleep now and we'll talk more about it in the morning."

I slammed the door behind me and stormed out carrying the suitcase in which I had packed all my clothes. "You wicked stray girl, what is there for you in Beirut anyway?" My grandmother insulted me from behind the iron lattice window. I kept on walking, toward what I hadn't seen yet, what I hadn't lived yet, the outside world. My grandmother was still standing in the same place, gripping the bars on the window. My aunt stood next to her, blinking violently and rallying all of the devils and demons of the earth against me. I didn't hate my aunt because I knew there was a small heart beating somewhere inside her chest. I knew that she too longed to open that door and slam it behind her. But she would never do it. Once I was out of their sight, she would turn to my grandmother and ask her to get back into her warm bed. Then she would go into the kitchen and make some hot soup for the old woman.

I sat in the ambulance that the Party had gotten from the Palestinians. We still called it the ambulance even though we used it to get around and deliver hospital supplies. It wasn't set up to transport the wounded because it moved at the pace of a turtle. The doctor renamed it "The Summer Headquarters" after it lost its back door. Its windows got smashed up one night during heavy shelling, too. The first time I rode in it down to Beirut didn't feel like the first time. I felt as though I was returning somewhere, going to see it again for the thousandth time. I vowed that it would never bore me. What went on there was all too real. The war there had another taste: more dangerous, truer, more powerful. I was certain that I was going to fall in love its abandoned, dilapidated buildings. The putrid stenches of the streets, mixed with the smells of blood, gunpowder, and death, suited me just fine. As for the violence awaiting me, I also awaited it with unflinching desire; I wanted to live to the utmost. Maybe, in that way, my soul would awaken from its deep malaise and I might begin to feel my body again, the body I sometimes had to pinch just to remember it was still there. Samer no longer amused me; neither did the late-night excursions in which we cruised the towns aimlessly, accompanied only by an insane screaming that expelled the fear growing inside all of us. Nothing changed between Akram and me. I no longer read any of his books but I did start philosophizing whenever I was around him, which confused him and caused him to lose his patience with me. He would start to yell and say how I saw the revolution from on high and that the truth was something else. When I think about him now, I imagine him roaming the city streets with piles of books tucked under his arm, holding onto them tightly, and with his other hand lifting his glasses, then replacing them over his anxious eyes just to read the street names. He fumbles around and is unable find the address he's looking for. I know that he won't know where to find me and that the young men, the town, my aunt, my grandmother, the hospital, Nawal, and the meetings are all still somewhere far, far away from my new home.

"This was just some idea you had and you made it happen," Muhammad said when I visited him in the hospital where he worked. "Come on, I'll bring you to my house. You can stay with me. My house isn't far from here. Besides, I spend most nights in the hospital anyway—ever since my family left I don't like sleeping in the house by myself."

Muhammad's house looked like him. It's strange how houses resemble their inhabitants. His house was full of colors and books. It seemed strange to me at first, but I got used to it. "You'll sleep in here," he told me, pointing to a small room with sky-blue walls. In one corner, two beds had been stacked on top of each other like two small wooden crates.

I reread the letter from my friend Leila inviting me to visit her in London. I read it aloud to Muhammad, who sat there listening. When he came back to the house that night, we went out together to buy some food. "I'm going to leave this country eventually," I said. "Go after the school year is over. Save yourself!" Muhammad said. I knew that he was giving me special attention. When he wrapped his arm around my shoulder, I was overtaken by a desire to move closer to him, to let him hold me close for a long time. This was different from the desire I used to have for Pierre, and which I only felt for a short time with Samer.

When he got home in the evening, Muhammad would come and kiss me on the cheek, asking if I was getting used to the school in the city I had enrolled in. Then he would embrace me and look at me for a while, disappointed, letting his arms fall to his sides, and say, "My God, you're still too young." "Too young for what?" I asked like a fool. "Am I too young to go to school, to study and live by myself in this city, or to hear the news that you bring home with you every night?"

Umm Fouad came by every Saturday morning. I would hear her open the door with the key she always kept with her. Before leaving, Muhammad would instruct her to be quiet so she wouldn't wake me up. Umm Fouad would clean the apartment and, after she had finished, offer me tea with a slice of cake that she made herself. I was amazed at how Muhammad used to fuss over me, spoiling me really. I used to drink tea in bed, cover up my head again and try to go back to sleep, enjoying the warmth and security.

Akram surprised me at the entrance to school one afternoon. He invited me to go with him to where the guys meet, a café near the Lebanese Arab University. Nawal also joined them, along with another young woman who I was meeting for the first time. In the Toledo Café, Akram introduced us to a man called Brother Yassine. Brother Yassine was going to teach us how to make Molotov cocktails. The man instructed us to leave the café and follow him, one at a time, leaving enough space between us so as not to arouse the suspicion of anyone passing by. We followed him to an apartment not far from the café. The elevator inside the gloomy building was out of order and its glass door was broken. The elevator shaft had become a trash bin and the gray walls of the stairwell were covered with slogans either written in a hurry or by the children who lived in the building: zigzagging and full of spelling mistakes.

The apartment was on the third floor. It was dark and besieged on all sides by large, looming buildings. We sat in a room with two couches that faced each other: one was upholstered with fabric dotted with large orange and green flowers; the other was the color of dark wine and its faded cloth cover was torn, and the cushions thrown on it were adorned with red Palestinian embroidery. There was a calendar from the year before still hanging on the wall, announcing the tenth of November. Brother Yassine sat in front of us on a small cotton cushion in the middle of the room.

He had brought an empty 7-Up bottle, a wick, and some explosive materials. A baby's crying drifted in from an adjoining room, then a woman started yelling. We heard the loud crack of a hand across a face, and another child began to cry. Brother Yassine continued his lecture on how to make a Molotov cocktail as if nothing had happened. When he finished, I thought about where I would ever be able to use such a bomb, if I decided to make it one day. I thought about my aunt but the thought immediately flew out of my head. I thought about Akram but banished the thought. I thought about those who shelled us every day without us ever knowing what their faces looked like. I told myself it would be impossible for me not to detonate the bottle in one of their faces. Otherwise, what was the point of everything I was learning, what good was the time I spent there? But no one came to mind and Brother Yassine didn't help me answer the question; he kept on talking about the Enemy without ever defining who that was exactly. He used to say: we hit the Enemy or we blew up one of the Enemy's cars.

"The next meeting will be in two days. Same time, same place. Don't forget," Akram said. "I won't," I said. "I'll drop you where you're staying." "No thanks," I said, before hurrying on ahead of him. I looked back and saw him still standing in the same place, watching me. I switched back just

to make him think that was the way to where I
was staying.

I had gone back to town the day before yesterday
because my grandmother had died. Only a few
people came to the funeral. Everyone was afraid
of the unpredictable shelling. Four pallbearers
carried her coffin. A man with the key to the
cemetery walked with them. They placed the
coffin on the roof of the car, secured it with ropes.
Then all five men got into the car and headed
toward the cemeteries at the base of town. The
sun would only be up at the base of town for a
little while longer. It's always cold there, even in
the middle of summer. When the peasants used
to come up to their houses from the deep valleys
at midday in the sweltering summer, they
hesitated for a bit at the cemeteries. They longed
to stop there, even if only for a few moments'
respite from the blistering sun. It was the only
place that stayed cool; it reminded them of early
springtime. But they never stopped there for long.
The dankness of the graves and the silence of the
dead frightened them.

I didn't cry when my grandmother died. I
didn't cry when I followed behind the car heading
to the cemetery either. No other girl wanted to
go with me. They said it was a place for men only
and that I should stay home. When I returned

home, I found my grandmother's bed empty. A mattress was still lying on it. The men had moved the corpse to the coffin, placed the shroud over it, and then had taken it far from her room. The women quickly turned the mattress over and folded it in half. This, they said, would stave off the evil eye. It was as though they wanted to send the dead far away from them. That night, my aunt slept in the same room where my grandmother's corpse had lain for a full day. My uncle slept in the other room, in the big bed, with his wife and son, who had accompanied him from Jordan. He was there by coincidence and not because of my grandmother's death. The next morning, my aunt put my grandmother's mattress out in the sun. She cleaned the room and wiped down the floor tiling, leaving the windows and doors open all day long.

"I want to travel!" I told my uncle, who didn't believe me. "Where to?" he asked. "I'll go abroad and continue my studies." "Fine, fine," he said, patting my back as though he could satisfy my desire by lying to me. He didn't realize the strength of my conviction. He thought I might change my mind. He hoped I would change my mind but he would be disappointed, as usual. His wife clucked, "You can enroll in the university here. You know that the money your mother sends you isn't nearly enough." My uncle's wife was holding her son, who was petrified of walking around barefoot. He said he was scared of cockroaches. I didn't respond, but I was filled with a momentary desire to see a massive army of cockroaches, cockroaches marching by and jumping all around her son, her son who was afraid of walking around barefoot. But my aunt, who had spent all day sweeping and mopping, didn't leave a single cockroach alive in the house, or anywhere nearby for that matter.

When I arrived in London, my friend Leila picked me up at the airport. She had gotten married four years earlier and moved there with her husband who worked for a Gulf magazine. Her husband used to come home early with a black leather briefcase. He placed a cigar in his mouth that he fiddled with constantly but rarely ever lit. I spent my first few days there sleeping. When Leila knocked on my door in the mornings, I told her it wasn't light out yet and asked why she was waking me up so early. "It's nine o'clock!" she said, laughing. Her house quickly emptied of people, emptied of her husband and emptied of her two children, who spent their mornings in the preschool nearby. I loved being in the house when it was just the two of us. That way, I was able to talk to her. How young my friend seemed. She was a very young mother. She had built a life for herself so quickly,

I thought. But the more I actually thought about it, the more I realized that she hadn't actually built her own life yet. She had cut short her studies for a spur-of-the-moment marriage and hadn't accomplished anything as she'd planned, including her plan not to have children for at least a few years.

When I got a job in London, I moved into a small room on the fourth floor of a building with no elevator. My place wasn't far from the Arabic radio station I worked for—a short dash I made every day on foot. I had to take the train every afternoon to the institute where I was studying translation.

During the six years I spent in London, I traveled abroad several times. I saw the world with my friend David, whom I'd met one night in a pub. We visited South Asia and Latin America together. All cities look the same, I would say to him. I want to meet real people, to talk to them. Wasting our time visiting museums and historical sites incensed me. I would stand there like an idiot with a tour group enthralled by ruins, all listening raptly to the tour guide's explanations. The guide went on and on while I nearly suffocated from the heat. David would listen avidly and I'd start to get annoyed. Just then, he'd point out a café nearby that he'd happened to notice. "Sweetie," he said, "why don't you go have a beer and wait for me over there?" In the evening,

when I wanted to go out dancing or walk through
the streets of the illuminated city, David would
demur, saying how sore his feet were, and
immediately fall asleep. I got used to going out
by myself. Sometimes I would call my Lebanese
friend Ibrahim, who was born in England, and
ask him to go out with me, while David stayed
home, passed out in front of the television set.

I used to tell myself that David was a nice
guy, that he loved me and that I just needed to
get used to living there. I repeated those very
words to myself even as the desire to move started
gnawing at me. When I told David that I didn't
feel safe there and I wanted to travel, he said he
was willing to sign over to me his house in
London or the piece of land he owned outside the
city. He didn't understand that my need for safety
was something else, that owning a house or land
wasn't going to change anything for me. "You
don't get it," I told him. "For God's sake, make
me understand, whatever I don't understand,
make me understand! I love you and want to
spend the rest of my life with you," he continued,
pacing back and forth in the living room. How
could he know what he wanted so clearly? I
wondered. He knew what he wanted from that
day until the day he died. Why were things so
easy for him? Why did I feel sometimes, when
we were waiting for the elevator, like I needed to
put my head on his shoulder and fall asleep, but

once we had entered the apartment, I would be assaulted by anxiety? Any drowsiness left me and I suddenly longed to go back outside. "For God's sake, what's gotten into you?" he asked me nervously. "Nothing, I just want to go back outside." David lost his patience and threw up his arms, as if to say that he couldn't do anything to stop me. "Go on, get out!" he repeated. I know that I may have appeared strong and upbeat but I also know that the whole time I was bleeding continuously somewhere within. I was trying to stanch the flow, pushing ahead as I was overwhelmed by one desire, the desire to move, to move and convince myself that I could be happy, that I'd finally find stability in this new place. But I quickly found out that it was just like all the other places I'd ever been. How was David going to understand all of this, when he approached me and my body remained cold, without any warmth at all? "Turn the light off," I told him, allowing my emptiness to fill back up. Then I started to think about Pierre. I imagined our sea voyage and the blazing sun burning between us. I told myself that Pierre was with me in that moment and sometimes his name came out among my labored breathing and the affectionate words I muttered as David kissed me.

In the pub near David's flat, I sat across from the bartender. He was mixing alcohol with fruit juice. He held the glass in his hands and stirred it.

The sound of the liquid mixing with the crushed ice was like passionate music from an equatorial country. "Oy, Camilia!" he said to me. "How're you? Weather's nice tonight." I finished my cup of coffee and glass of cognac quickly. I called my friend Ibrahim at home but there was no answer. I went out, I didn't feel like going back home yet. I walked through the empty streets. What if the war broke out here, too? I asked myself. What if the dignified buildings of London and the train stations exploded? Why don't wars happen in cities like this? Why do wars only seem to be happening in cities that look like ours? I crossed the street again and headed toward David's apartment. I opened the door. I found him sleeping. I saw his face, peaceful like a baby's.

"Will you come with me to Beirut?" my friend Ibrahim, who was studying filmmaking, asked me. "I want to make my first film about the street fighters. You could come with us, with John and me. John helps me film and you'd make a good guide and translator for us since you're from there. I can't promise you much, just a plane ticket and accommodation. You'll have to take care of the rest."

"I'm going to help Ibrahim make his film." That's what I told David as I said goodbye to him at Heathrow. "Write to me," he said, waving his hand. I nodded, knowing that I wasn't going to write. I hadn't written anyone for a very long time. Ever since I realized that the letters I wrote to my mother and the red hearts I drew for her when I was little were pointless and that she was never coming back. The telephone is an amazing invention, I thought to myself. "I'll call you," I shouted to David and then climbed onto the escalator.

The war hadn't totally destroyed the city—it seemed that what I'd seen on British television about the war in Beirut wasn't entirely accurate. For a while, I'd even believed that there were no longer any houses left standing and that anyone who hadn't died yet had been abandoned in the shelters and hadn't been able to move since the last battle started. The city hadn't changed. The few places I'd seen before leaving had become even more crowded. But the war went on and people continued having children, buying cars and houses, and walking down the street. The road we took from the airport in to the city was an earthy brown. I opened my suitcases at the airport for inspection and opened them again on the street when the car was stopped at one of the many checkpoints that had sprung up all over the place.

Most of the houses in my hometown had been destroyed. Other houses had been built haphazardly, houses that had been quickly filled with families. Their construction seemed likely to collapse at any moment and their outer walls were left unpainted. My aunt wasn't there anymore. She had moved to a safer town deep in the heart of the mountains. The top floor of our house had been destroyed. No one lived on the ground floor anymore. Therese had emigrated to Canada with her husband and young son. I stood in front of Ibrahim while he panned around toward me. I climbed the staircase with the collapsed sides. "Careful!" he shouted. I climbed up and motioned for him to follow. "Come on, I want you to see where I slept when I was little." We reached the entrance to the house. The glass of the wrought-iron window had been shattered, and through it I could see what remained of our damaged possessions. Whatever furniture was still intact had been moved to the ground floor. The house was locked. No one could open the iron front door anymore. Shrapnel had damaged the lock and mangled its metal: locked places that keys couldn't open. I saw children playing soccer near the house. One of them took a shot and the ball flew high into the air before landing on the balcony of one of the half-destroyed and abandoned houses. He climbed up on the balcony, picked up the ball and threw it down to where the rest of them began fighting for it. From the middle of the street, someone told us to get moving because the bombing usually started around sundown. Someone else said that he knew me from my aunt's stories, that she still came by every once in a while to inspect the house and the field. Outside, there was a single rose in a planter with a blossom that unfolded into purple, gently trembling in the breeze.

The field hospital had been moved from its original location to another, two-story building. It had grown and had been made more secure. I wasn't going to visit my aunt in the nearby town. She thought I was still abroad.

We returned to Beirut in the early evening. The driver didn't take the main road to the capital. He took a different one that I wasn't familiar with. Snipers threatened the roads I'd always known. What am I doing here? I asked myself. What had I been doing back there in that other country? "If it wasn't for this film, I would go back tonight," I told Ibrahim, fighting back my tears. "Back where?" he asked me. "I don't know," I said. When we reached the hospital at the end of the Corniche, in the heart of the city, I told the driver to hang a right. "I'll introduce you to a friend I haven't seen for a long time," I told Ibrahim. The narrow street that intersects the main road near Dr. Muhammad's house had been entirely blocked off with piles of sandbags. He used to call me "my little one." I imagined the look on his face when he saw me. I knew I hadn't changed at all, except for my hair, which I had let grow long like my uncle had always wanted me to. "You can stay with me until you find a place," Muhammad said, embracing me. Muhammad's face had changed and his hair had gone completely white. He had shaved his mustache and he looked a little wider. He'd gained that little extra something that men get when they begin the second half of their lives.

I spent that month exploring Beirut, getting to know it better. Nadim gave me the address of a friend of his named Maha. He told me I could stay with her if I wanted. First, I wanted to see where she lived. That way I could hold onto the money Ibrahim had given me to rent a room. I went to meet her. I told Nadim over the phone that I would need a day to make up my mind. The place was depressing and not at all what I had expected. The woman was silent and didn't ask me any questions. When she learned that I was staying at Muhammad's, she said she knew him well and that he was an old friend of hers. And now I have one more home, I thought, chuckling. I moved some of my clothes and belongings over to Maha's apartment. All my stuff had been scattered between Ibrahim's place and John's place, and now Muhammad's apartment as well.

"Calm down, have a seat," Muhammad said. "What are you looking for?" "I'm not looking for

anything. I'm just retracing my steps from the
front door." "Before you start making the film,
you really have to get to know the city. Does it
make any sense for you to shoot a film about a
city you know nothing about?" he asked me,
incredulously. I sat across from him, folding and
crossing my legs as though I had practiced yoga
for a long time. I listened to him as he went on
talking. I listened hoping that what he was saying
might help me connect to this place. Muhammad
talked. I saw the city in front of me. The keys of
my imagination opened all its doors. I saw its
colors and smelled its scents. When the flow of
conversation dried up, its image remained
suspended in my mind's eye. It persisted in the
moments stretching out between wakefulness and
sleep. The images lingered and then I closed my
eyes, waiting for another blaze of light to come
to me. Further conversation restarted my breath
and awakened my slumbering limbs.

We went out and my friend Ibrahim hoisted
the camera onto his shoulder and brought his face
in close to the eyepiece. We followed the dirt road
from in front of the bombed-out hotel. The sea
appeared clearly behind us; so did our car, which
was parked near the pool of the hotel, which had
also been abandoned.

"Where's the statue?" I asked when we
reached Beshara al-Khoury Street. "The statue
was blown up," said Maha, "but the name stuck."

There were many places where only the names were left. There were other places where the names had acquired new meanings. The statue was blown up; the statue toppled. Other statues were erected in different places. Monuments shooting up toward the sky: despite their average height, they seemed to loom over our heads, constricting our breathing. "The statues rose up against us," said Maha, who only made that one comment throughout the entire trip. "Against us, against us," my friend holding the camera repeated in a soft stammer, searching for a rhythm. Then he started inventing words, trying to make up a song, freestyle, but he couldn't seem to get it going. When a woman in a short skirt passed by, he let out a long whistle, shoving his face up against the car window and whistling the national anthem, which a shopkeeper near Muhammad's apartment had taught him. He didn't get the tune quite right and the woman didn't stop to look at him; she kept on walking slowly ahead, admiring the clothes on display in one of the glass storefronts. "Once ain't enough," I told him, smiling. "Another one ain't enough," he added.

"I want to go back to the hotel," Ibrahim said. "No, it's too soon to go back. Come on, I want to show you a local restaurant." I had eaten lunch there with Muhammad the day before. "First let's stop by the hotel to get some more film," said my friend, who I rewarded with a brief, stolen kiss for his spontaneity. Maha believed that I had nowhere to go and I never once tried to convince her otherwise. Every place is mine.

I told Maha that I was going to the South for a couple of days. I was away for a full week, and when I came back, she was gone. There was a knock at the door. It was Ranger, the fighter I'd met in front of the building when I first came to visit Maha. He reeked of sweat, had a rough chin and there were traces of gunpowder on his fingers. I found Muhammad's news of the city amusing. Sometimes I thought I knew this city, that I really knew it. Maybe I had even lived in it once; maybe I was born and raised there in a past life. It was as though I had already seen everything he was telling me, as though I had heard it all before or even lived all of its details and events. These stories awakened my desire for a paradise I could only dream of but had never experienced. Ranger told me his stories, too, his fresh-off-the-street stories: their smells wrapped around our noses and lingered in our rooms. The smells of his stories were like his smells: harsh, without mercy. In his harshness, I could see absolute and unambiguous pride. His stories were sharp, like chronic pain that had no cure. They rained down on my head like painful blows, but they also made me want to hear more, a desire more powerful than any talk. I listened to Ranger, who I had started seeing everyday, an addiction I couldn't shake. Ranger would come over and not leave; then he and I would stay in together, not going out for days at a time. "I don't understand you," Maha said, after I came back from a two-day getaway spent with Muhammad. "How are you capable of this?" she asked me. "I understand your relationship with Muhammad, but why Ranger too?" I answered her in a perfected reflex, as though I had anticipated her question: "My relationship with Ranger is necessary for the film I'm working on, of course." I was lying to her, telling myself that she would never understand that Muhammad and Ranger were my whole world, that they were two ends of a pole that I held in the middle to help me carefully walk across a high wire. I held the pole level and straight, stepped forward like an acrobat afraid of losing his balance and falling.

Muhammad told me about Beirut, this city that mattered to him but that I couldn't see. "My city is different," he said. "Your children destroyed your city," I told him. "My children have nothing to do with it. They're in France with their mother." He understood what I meant to say, but he ignored it all the same. He looked left and right, as though searching for something that he had lost. "I don't have any children here," he continued. "Don't try and deceive me. Look at me. Look me in the eye. Maybe if it weren't for the fathers of those kids, the war would never have broken out..." I said. "I don't know, maybe," Muhammad mumbled with plain disinterest.

In the middle of the night, one night when I couldn't sleep, Muhammad started talking about the city again: its people and its crowdedness; its sites, music, and art; the cafés it once had; its theater; its meetings, politics, and conversation; and its interminable night. "I don't know this city you're describing at all," I told him. "It's not mine. You're talking about some other city that doesn't look like my city at all. But all cities look the same. They look the same in times of peace and they look the same in times of war." "Beirut doesn't look like other cities," Muhammad said. "It has always been in a state of readiness, for whatever was going to happen. Even as one day ends something unknown is being prepared for the next. Things happen and change the face of the city."

I didn't know what would happen to Muhammad and me. He wanted to grow old in peace and I wanted to reclaim some unknown place he had always told me about, to reclaim that place in a single moment, as though I had inhabited it for many years. The twenty years that separated me from Muhammad vanished whenever he talked to me. He used to sparkle when he was talking. His eyes were luminous, like fire in a pitch-black night; I could only see this in moments, inadvertently. The places he described sounded vaguely familiar, as though I'd heard it all before. Then I started asking myself whether I had actually seen those places or if I had just constructed images in my mind from all that I'd heard about them, and then they became part of my memory.

I don't know why Muhammad cried whenever he had an orgasm with me. He would bury his head in my bosom and say how he wished he could be my age again and love me in a different way. I told myself that he cried for some other reason that he refused to tell me about. He asked me to play the new Fairuz song for him over and over, the only song he ever wanted to hear. He didn't want to listen to any other songs from the cassettes. He drew close to me, saying, "You're my woman, you're my woman from now on." In these moments, I would ask myself what I was doing there. Why was I trying to reconstruct a lost place with a man who had a chance to make his revolution but failed? Since then, he'd searched for comfort in me, someone who herself could find none.

My friend Ibrahim still suffers from great pain in his shoulder where the militiaman slugged him and snatched his camera in the middle of the city. After a drawn-out negotiation, the camera was returned, but the film was gone. "I lost two whole days of filming," Ibrahim said despondently. "You lost two whole days?" Muhammad asked him with unmitigated scorn. "That's such a long time. They stole two whole days from you!" Muhammad squinched up his face and his eyes to convey sarcastic pity. "We haven't lost any time at all, just fifteen years!" He fell silent for a moment and then raised his voice so that the sarcasm would be even more biting: "What miserable luck you have! Can you imagine how many rolls of film you could have filled in fifteen years? Go on, just try and count them all!" Muhammad approached me and whispered, "I have a mind to open the door and throw your considerate friend right out. Just look at how we've lost our lives and how our wars have spilled into the streets and back alleys. And along comes a man like your friend here who tries to gather up everything we've lost into a single film. He records our fragility and our fear. He puts all of that on film, just a movie."

"I feel like giving my gun some practice," said Muhammad. "Like taking it out of storage. To stand on the balcony and *Ta! Ta! Ta!* To open fire on the street, on the people, on the cats passing by and the stray dogs." I asked him why. He jabbed his finger against his temple and said: "Because I feel like it, that's why." Maha asked him, "And those people, what's their crime? Those passing by on the street, they're like you, most of them are displaced." "That's a lie," Muhammad said. "They're all nothing but liars. They come to the hospital telling everyone about their displacement, about their hardships. They're just looking for sympathy and I don't have sympathy for anyone anymore. Sometimes I wonder why they didn't just die in their houses, why the bombs didn't just pick them off one by one, why they came to the city only to fill its streets and buildings with their shouting, their smells and their dead. They destroyed its buildings and filled it with sorrow." "But this is war," Maha interrupted him by saying, "The war destroyed their houses and they've had years taken from their lives. People leave destruction behind and flee even as the war rages on. Men's fingers stay on the trigger while women look for safe places for their children." Muhammad laughed, and once he started laughing, he wouldn't stop. His eyes started watering and then I started to laugh at his laughter. "My God, don't ever change," he said to Maha. "Stay the way you are and you'll stay like that till the end of your life. War is war. Come on, tell me what the war accomplished?" Muhammad asked her. "A life of misfortune is unfortunate with or without war. But at least the war has amused us a little. Maybe we would have died of

boredom without it. It made us wait and wait. I
came back to Beirut to work as a doctor for the
revolution. I started sleeping in the hospital, eating
in the hospital. I stopped seeing my wife and after
two years she said she couldn't handle living here
anymore. She took our two kids and went back to
her country. Where's the revolution? The only
revolution since the Bolshevik is the Porno-
graphic. That's the real revolution, honey. It would
have been better for me to stay far away from here,
to keep on dreaming, waiting to return." "Shut up!
My God, you're delirious, my head hurts from all
of your blathering," I said. Maha muttered
something incomprehensible and shook her head
as if to say that she disagreed. She blinked several
times and then looked at Muhammad. After a
while, she asked, "Are you coming back with me or
are you staying here?" "I'm staying here," I replied.

At night, we took the road down to the
Corniche. The streets were dark. Muhammad
was driving. Sitting in the back seat, Maha stared
out the window and remained silent.

"I love the city like this, naked like birth, like
death," I said.

"I love nakedness, too," Muhammad joked.
"Especially without the philosophy."

"I'm afraid of the city changing. I don't know
another side of it. I've gotten used to the holes in
its walls, which are huge eyes seeing nothing but
the death of the hero, his last demise."

"Heroes never die here," said Maha, "only we die." Then, after a moment, she added, "And I'm afraid of dying."

"I'm not afraid of dying," I answered her, "but I'm afraid of going crazy, of staying alive, deranged…"

"Wouldn't it be so much better to be born as an old man and die as a child?" Muhammad asked. "Maybe, that way, we could make our peace with death and then begin to wait for it, as though it were all just a game."

The driver dropped us someplace near the checkpoint this morning. "I'll leave you guys here. You can get a car to the other side," the driver said. "Someone's waiting for us over there," I replied to reassure him. Ibrahim and I crossed to the other side. John was waiting for us. He had been staying at the Alexander Hotel. He said he was afraid to cross over because of his blonde hair and blue eyes. The only time he had ever crossed here, he put on a hat and glasses, thinking that no one would recognize him as a foreigner. After handing back his press pass and vigorously patting him on the shoulder, pushing him forward a little bit, the young man at the checkpoint told him, laughing, "Even if you disguised yourself in a thousand different costumes, we'd still be able to spot you a mile

away. Move along, move on, and don't be afraid."
When John walked on, the fighter stared after
him. Then he looked at us, winked and said, "He's
hot like the girls." "A real hottie," commented
another militiaman sitting near the sandbags. I
know that fighter, I told Ibrahim. I had met him
once before when I was with Ranger.

The city was no different on the other side. It
looked the same everywhere. I didn't even notice
that we had crossed over until I saw the massive
piles of sandbags and the hordes of armed men
and weapons. We left our old place, where the
women all wrapped in cloaks as dark as night had
assembled. The faces of the young men at the
checkpoint resembled the faces of those that we'd
left behind in the other neighborhood. When I
told them what I was thinking, one of the
journalists waiting with John for us commented
that this area was cleaner and that he didn't see
any foreigners in the street, or any beggars either.
I cruised the city from West to East. There are
statues back there like the statues over here. *They
died so that Lebanon might live*, I read under one of
the posters pasted to the wall. I translated what I
read for Ibrahim, who commented drowsily,
"They died but Lebanon still didn't live." He
picked up the camera. "Hang on a sec!" he said to
the man behind the wheel. He filmed for a few
minutes, put the camera beside him and started
to whistle a slow melody.

I translated in real time the interview that John had conducted with one of the military leaders in East Beirut. The most dedicated, select military society occupied the large building by the port. I couldn't feel anything but incapacitating fear in such a place. But John seemed comfortable there and sure of himself. He was totally protected. I was the frightened one and I started chattering as I never had before. I prattled on in English and purposefully pronounced the words in a broken way to demonstrate that I had just stepped off the boat.

In the seaside café outside the capital, the journalist with us found a place near the window that stretched across the café's entire western side, looking out onto the coastal road. The tables near the window were always full, filled with the sort of people who love to sit cafés and look out the window. The place was like an observation room made of glass, except that those sitting inside were regarding life going on outside. They didn't believe that there was anything worth looking at inside. Above the door separating the two rooms, there was a picture of a military leader raising a glass and smiling. He seemed to be toasting those sitting down, joining them in drinking to their health. We didn't stay very long. We ordered a bunch of beers and took them to the car with us. "So we're carrying on to the North?" I asked. "No, we'll go North tomorrow," Ibrahim said, yawning.

"Fine! It's all in God's hands, I'll go with you then," I said to John. "Can you guarantee some modest digs for me in your grand hotel?"

Muhammad used to keep me around in his apartment with his conversation. He kept me around in the absence of his wife and kids. For a few brief moments, I decided that I was going to stop looking for somewhere else, that I was going to stay put in this city, which was still looking for its own place. He kept me around with conversation. Is there anything else in this city besides conversation that could make me stay? But what outfit would I dress my soul in? What kind of relationship would I forge through conversation? A relationship that floated away at the slightest breeze, with a little gust of boredom, that flew away like his small talk, which came out but was never reciprocated. Muhammad gathered up conversation, picked it like olives, styled it like my grandmother's hair, buttoned it up, and then filled the palm of my hand with it. I spread my hand out before me and the individual letters making up his conversation flew away like an angel that had just carried out its mission and departed. I would stay with him. We planned our romantic rendezvous to fit with my lifestyle and with lifestyle of a man who had another woman somewhere in this world, the life of a man who went on and on about a lost city. Very little planning, I thought. Our lives righted themselves and continued on their way But could I stay? I banished the question from my head. I didn't want to think, too much thinking made my head hurt. I supposed that my days were proceeding without too much suffering and for that, I should have been grateful. We planned our rendezvous and our times for telling stories about a place that I never knew. He tempted me with the art of conversation, describing a paradise I'd never dreamed of. He rolled out a carpet of desire and yearning before me that led to a forbidden place. If I desired that place, then I desired him and especially him. Isn't that what desire is, what love is: to search for something but never find it? But what good does it do me to desire a place without ever being able to live there? A curse washed over me, like rivers running over at winter's end.

Maha

There was nowhere left for me on the face of the earth but my apartment. I didn't leave it throughout the entire war. Besides, with all my landlord's attempts to evict me, why would I finally give in? He accused me of being a Communist. What he meant: I'm a whore for having a lot of men over. I did have a lot of men over, in fact, but they were just friends. At first, I used to pay the rent every month. His wife would come over to pick it up in his Fiat. She was a beautiful woman who made every effort to look elegant and who always tried to hide her fat behind beneath a flowing, silk shirt. Sometimes he knocked on the door instead, greeting me with a smile as he smoked a small cigar. He extended one hand to shake mine and patted my shoulder with the other, saying, "By

God, you're like a sister to me." Then he let his hand slide, heavy and sticky, down the length of my arm. Whenever I spied his red round face through the small peephole, I would start getting the money ready so I could thrust it out to him the moment I opened the door.

Back then, the neighborhood was more alive, more bustling, and I was called comrade. I don't know how things changed exactly. The Israelis came, marched through the streets of Beirut, breathing a lot of our air. Then they left. As the years went by, people started calling me a *hurma*. A lot of things happened but I didn't bother asking why or trying to find some kind of connection to tie it all together. A long time passed in which I didn't see my landlord. I started giving the rent to the doorman instead. I didn't recognize my landlord's wife on the day she came up and greeted me in front of the entrance. Her body was wrapped in a flowing caftan and her head was wrapped in a brightly colored silk scarf.

I spent many days in the shelter. The four-story building hadn't been emptied of its inhabitants yet; the doorman and his family hadn't left their dank room to take shelter in his village yet, either. In the shelter, I would amuse myself by eavesdropping on other people's conversations: news distracted me from the sound of the bombs. I set my imagination free and came up with my own ending to the stories I heard, which were then woven into the fabric of my memory and my dreams. The people's stories blended together throughout the day. Sometimes as people left the shelter to go back up to their apartments, the stories went with them. At night, the shelter would change and most people slept. The places that belonged to particular families there rolled up and shrunk as though disappearing inside themselves. Corners became the property of whoever occupied them, the property of women, as if they were extensions of their homes, of their bedrooms and their kitchens. Every family claimed borders for itself, imaginary boundaries. Every corner became a place belonging to someone, enclosed by propped-open suitcases. Shoes piled up near the one-gallon water tanks, which soaked the ground underneath them. Bodies moved closer together at night. They moved closer together and then went limp. Children mumbled in their sleep. Some of their voices came out imitating the sounds of explosions. *Tar... taq... tar... taq*, Lilian's son Karim repeated in his sleep. The man inhabiting the farthest corner sought some privacy by hanging up a large wool blanket and feigning a sharp cough whenever he made love to his wife behind it. Her moans were disguised by other sounds she made on purpose; she flailed her arms around, making the golden bangles covering her wrists clang together, for example. Lilian, my friend and neighbor who lived on the third floor, looked at me and whispered, with a puckish smile on her face, "I think I've forgotten how to do that." At that moment, the man's cough acquired a noticeably turned-on quality and sped up into comically heavy breathing.

Before, I used to be afraid at night. During the day, when the sun was strong and cast a belt of its rays on the walls of my apartment, I wasn't afraid. Life changed, everything changed, and I got used to the violent chaos outside. I no longer jumped out of bed in a panic to hurry down to the shelter. Instead, I adjusted my lifestyle to a violence that almost swallowed me whole. I came to have a makeshift bed near the apartment entry and another down in the shelter. This adjustment didn't make me feel any less forlorn or improve my dulled taste for things. There were many things I had stopped doing, things that had lost all meaning. Also, Noosa, my little cat, stopped jumping up on the bed to curl up with me and purr near my feet. She chose a small corner in the kitchen where she went to take comfort in the warmth of the refrigerator motor, even though there was no longer any electricity. I tried to make her understand that the big white box was no longer functioning, but she didn't understand at all. Josefa squeezed my wrist whenever a strange feeling of being strangled came over me. All my desires and the fervent pulse of life that had once resided in me were gone. I told her, "Massage my wrist well," as if air entered my lungs from there. The words came from deep inside me, broken. They came out like whistling wind released from the throat, escaping as incomprehensible fragments. Josefa massaged my wrists hard, until the tempo of my breathing started to come down and become more regular. She splashed water on me, then she massaged the upper part of my chest with oil that she had heated over the fire. In her Spanish accent, she told me, "Cover yourself well. There's a draft in here." I continued welcoming the rising sun each and every morning but it never reached my empty soul; it collided with my windowsill and stopped right there.

Ghassan died but he was still fixed in my breath and in my soul. I was overwhelmed by a desire to see him. In the narrow space between sleep and wakefulness, he would return to me. I smelled his scent. I reclaimed the heat of his breath as if it were a tattoo inscribed in my flesh. "I'm just a drop in the ocean," he used to tease me. "Some day I'll be reborn in another body and come back to you." His eyes sparkled before he went back to rubbing his face in my hair.

Many things happened since then. The war changed; it became another war. Sometimes it occurs to me that perhaps it didn't change after all, but rather, we changed and we no longer cared for it. My life and the life all around me changed. Houses that had once been filled with love were emptied of their inhabitants. Spaces lost the intimacy of conversation that used to warm them amid the long nights of shelling. I used to ask myself what happened that summer and what happened afterward. But things moved along quickly and my questions could no longer keep up. The stories people told in the shelters weren't amusing anymore; they became boring because of their constant repetition.

My grandmother passed away. Her last days had been miserable. She stopped recognizing anyone. She started calling me by my mother's name and found it hard to believe that I was actually her granddaughter Maha. She peed on the floor next to her bed and no one but Umm Mansour was around to take care of her. She left me her *qabu* in the mountains: a single spacious room big enough for her possessions: couches, beds, a wardrobe and another cabinet for the china, a small table and some chairs. Even after she passed away, the *qabu* furnishings were left adorned with the embroidered fabrics and small blankets that my grandmother had made assiduously throughout her life.

My neighborhood in the city had changed. I saw lots of people looking down from the balconies of houses that weren't theirs. Their clothes gave away the fact that they had recently moved to the city from somewhere far away; so did their boorish shouting, loud music, and the strange smells that emanated from their kitchens through broken windows and lingered in the narrow back streets; the smells in the neighborhood changed. Even the shopkeepers began to stock their shelves with goods I had never seen before that I didn't know how to use. When I asked for something I used to buy before the war started, they told me that it could no longer be found in the country, that no one bought it anymore. The vegetable sellers would come early in the morning and then slip away before the streets got boisterous and the shelling started up again.

Behind the building, the garden with palm, pomegranate, and orange trees became a parking lot for military vehicles. The trees had been uprooted from the center of the garden. Military vehicles stood in their place. The trunks of the trees that once blanketed the building walls and climbed up to our balcony had been destroyed and dried up without us even noticing. Maybe trees also feel pain when they are snapped and when they dry up, but they die like poets: silent and alone.

The space for play narrowed. The children who used to play in the garden had to retreat into the building. Their world was overrun by games played by grownups who didn't actually like to play. The kids gathered in the cramped lobby at the entry to the building, near the out-of-order elevator, shouting at each other, copycatting war games with weapons they made out of wood and then running up the stairs to their mothers, whose clothes smelled like fresh food. The neighborhood no longer resembled the neighborhoods in the cities of other countries. In front of the building entrance—a place of perpetual danger—the children's shouting rang out, filling up the hours of the day. The children here differed from children in other cities, too. There, the apartments were devoid of children's voices, which filled the schools all day.

Most of the families that had lived in the building for many years had fled the neighborhood and left me their keys. Lilian and Talal went to their hometown in the South and gave me the keys to the other apartments. When Lilian came back, she didn't stay long before deciding to flee the country. I became the keymaster. That's what Lilian, the last one to leave the building, called me as she bid me farewell and left.

A short time went by before new families moved into the building, families we'd never seen in the neighborhood before. Families also appeared in the surrounding buildings. The intensity of the war in the South increased. The war sprouted up in other regions. War here, war there: the war here seemed more familiar, as though people had grown accustomed to it and no longer bothered to run from it. People hung their clothes up to dry from their living room balconies. Clothes of all different seasons and all different ages were mixed together; clean colorful clothes flapped in the breeze as the wind spattered water droplets onto the balconies below, onto the streets covered with sand from the checkpoints that had been set up at both ends. Families with many old people, old people who wore the same clothes year round. People brought their elders with them; they brought them and all their possessions; they sat them down where the whole family could see them, in the middle of homes they had barged into without keys. Maybe that was so they wouldn't forget about their elders if they happened to sit somewhere out of sight.

"I'm Nadim's friend, Camilia," the young woman hastened to tell me when I opened the front door of my apartment for her. It was impossible not to be struck by her face. It had been a long time since I had seen a face so full of life. It had been a long time since I had opened the front door for a visitor at all. Who was this woman? What did she want from me? Why did she choose to come to my apartment? In that moment, there was no

choice but to step back in time, back to a time
when eyes still shimmered, when our faces awoke
to mornings bursting with questions—Where?
What? When? How? Why? Especially why.
I'm Nadim's friend, Camilia. Did she actually
say that? Nadim! I hadn't seen him for so long.
After Ghassan died, he came by to offer his
condolences. He sat across from me, then he
moved his chair closer to hold my hand in both of
his and just sat there, silent. The woman was still
standing by the door staring at me, waiting for
me to invite her in. Just then, I was struggling
hard to recall what Ghassan's face looked like. I
went back and dug it out from all the other faces
that had piled up in my memory. I opened the
door halfway, just enough for her to squeeze
inside. No one had knocked on my door for a
long time. What friends of mine were still around
had become too afraid to come and visit me in
this neighborhood. *Whoever comes in is lost in vain
and whoever goes out is born again*: That's how
Ghassan described our neighborhood during the
early years of the war, and that's how he went on
describing it.

I was alone until the moment that young
woman walked through my door. Now I say that
I was alone, but I didn't feel that way at the time.
That may have been because I was so
disconnected from my own life, in a way that
bodily presence became no different than

absence. I was thinking about all of that when I asked this visitor to back away from the window and move to a safer place inside the apartment. She had come to Beirut from England to shoot a film about the life of the militiamen on the street and about those who continued living along the frontlines. What took her so long? I thought, derisively. And what hadn't been filmed already in this city? She approached me and sat down on the small chair I had placed near the kitchen door. I stared at her. This was the first chance I'd had to really look at her since she'd come in. Her brown hair was held back in a braid by a bronze barrette, she had no makeup on her face except for a thin black line of eyeliner. It was clear that hers was the kind of beauty that didn't require much work to be shown off, like a wild flower that hadn't yet been picked. She was petite and radiant. "You live in a dangerous area!" she said. Without looking at me, she added, "It's hard to get around here under such conditions." It seemed that she had started to wonder how she was going to get back while the shelling was still going on. But I decided not to get myself mixed up in any kind of relationship; she was never going to stay with me anyway, so her predicament didn't concern me one bit. That's what I decided. The young lady repeated that she had come to shoot a film about the fighters of the city streets and that Nadim had given her my address. Fuck you, my friend! I thought. She was articulate and spoke naturally, from time to time biting the long pearl necklace she wrapped around her fingers while she talked. Her eyes sparkled with the ferocity of a flame. The longer she went on talking, the more my doubts about whether I actually wanted her to stay in my house increased. When she got up to go to the kitchen and make herself a cup of Nescafé, she asked if I wanted one, too, as if she had lived here a long time. "I know all about you," she said, before adding, "Nadim told me all about you the last time we saw each other in England." She handed me a mug and, in that moment, I felt a kind of intimacy I hadn't had for a long time. I heard myself saying, "As long as the shelling continues, you'll stay here. We'll wait and see what else you can do tomorrow."

She pulled a nightgown and a toothbrush out of her handbag. She looked at me, smiling as though she could sense the confusion in my eyes, and said, "I carry my toiletries with me wherever I go." Her nightgown was pink with a white fringe that hung down from the lace collar and the sleeves. I moved closer and touched the shirt with my fingertips. It was satiny and smooth to the touch. It had been a long time since I wore a nightgown. I didn't need anyone to remind me of things like that, of how instinct was no longer enough to protect me, to keep me passionate about life. But how could instinct alone be enough to defend us when we had neglected so many things?

When I woke up the next morning, I found that Camilia had woken up long before me. Fairuz's voice was streaming from the small radio: songs that made me feel like I was still waiting in the train station and had been for years; songs I loved but that always made me sad. The aroma of piping-hot Nescafé drifted out of the kitchen. Camilia appeared bearing a large serving tray with breakfast on it. She placed the tray on the table she'd already brought outside. "Come on out, let's have breakfast on the balcony. The sun is nice this morning," she said. Taking a sip from her mug, she added, "This is the life, isn't it?"

That morning, one of the neighborhood militiamen came and asked us to go down to the shelter, "because we're about to start shelling from here." The young lady absurdly protested against those who were making war: "At least wait until we've finished our breakfast!" Camilia responded to the absurdity of war with her own, inadvertent absurdity. Camilia looked at him, smiled, and added, "Just give us ten minutes." What was this madness that we lived? I watched, expecting the fighter's rage to explode in Camilia's face at any moment, but he didn't do anything of the sort. He took a piece of bread spread with apricot jam from her, tossed it in his mouth and hurried back outside.

Boredom was consuming my life, while this young woman projected vigor and passion. When she told me she had an aunt who lived outside the city and that she was looking for a place to spend the last few months while she finished shooting the film, I found myself telling her that she could stay with me, that there was enough room for two. After closing the apartment door behind me, I stood on the balcony and watched her come out of the building and head toward the end of the street, light as a butterfly floating on the wind. She told me she would come back after she had picked up her things. I waited a long time for her. Whenever a bomb went off, my heart skipped a beat and I went to look out the window. Then I went out onto the balcony barefoot. When a car pulled up and stopped in front of the building, I told myself that it had to be her, that someone must be dropping her off because of the amount of stuff she had brought with her.

Days went by and this woman was still in my house. I soon forgot what I had promised myself about not getting too involved with anyone else on the face of the earth. My silence was a tacit agreement to let her stay as long as she liked. She had taken over my house and conferred upon it her own, intimate smells. Her presence altered my modest space. My house changed even if its address did not. My possessions no longer had permanent places and I didn't want to resist how things were changing. I was like someone drowning who surrendered to being swept away by the movement of the waves.

It seemed as though she'd never given up the habits that I had stopped. Different in every way, that's how she seemed to me, a difference that increased my usual anxiety with her vivacious mood. She started looking for water and found it in plastic containers that I'd placed in the corner of the kitchen. "A cold shower can stimulate your circulation," she said, and then added from the bathtub, screaming as she poured the water over her head, "but I can't take it!" The candle on the edge of the tub cast faint, dancing shadows on her face and body as she leaned forward. Her face seemed sallower than it should have been. When she took off her cotton shirt, shadows flickered on her naked body and were thrown onto the cold bathroom walls. She closed the door halfway and jumped into the tub like a gleeful little girl, giggling as the cold surprised her. She poured the water over her body and shrieked, lathering herself with a sponge dripping with soapsuds. I was sitting beside three candles, staring at a book open in front of me but I wasn't reading. I was listening to the abbreviated songs that Camilia was singing one after the other, leaning her head forward so her voice would resonate, slow and deep, as though coming from a record that had been ground down from being overplayed.

That evening, the sounds began to recede from the streets adjacent to ours. I planned to sleep in my room. I missed that. I spread whatever candles were left around the bedroom. Camilia came in with her wet hair wrapped in a towel that she had taken without asking, humming a classic tune. Her nightgown hung on her like a paper bag. She was joyful amid the sorrow that enveloped my life.

Sometimes, distant sounds woke me. The sounds of endlessly falling rain reached me through the window near my bed. I raised my head a little bit so that I could hear better and guess the distance between the location of the explosions and me. Night blanketed the space outside, a night without borders. When the sounds increased in number, it became impossible for me to distinguish between the sound of thunder and the sound of an explosion. The sounds of the explosions blended with the sound of the rain. I had a greater tolerance for the sounds when the rain was falling, as if the explosions got wet in the rain, grew softer and became less harsh on the walls of the houses and their inhabitants. In the early dawn, I woke Camilia up and we went to sleep in the entryway. Camilia crossed the distance between the bedroom and the entryway with her eyes closed,

as though sleepwalking. I held her hand so she
wouldn't bump into the things strewn all around
her. As soon as her head was on the pillow, she
fell into a deep sleep. I couldn't sleep. I sat on the
foam mattress spread out on the ground. The call
of the muezzin rang out, followed by the voice of
another muezzin. The sounds blended with
booming explosions that seemed to be moving
farther away. The voice of the muezzin burned
away my fear of what I lived through at night and
assured me that morning was inevitably coming.
The word "Allah" spread out and elongated in
precisely the same moment that my lungs
expanded. Air pierced my chest and the chronic
pain jolting through my wrists like lightning
disappeared. The word expanded to cover the
horizon at dawn, sparkling like a thin veil of light.
As the words got closer together, my heart
drowned and those thunderous sounds came
back, bellowing like deaf wild creatures.

I fell asleep for a little while but when I
awoke, Camilia was nowhere to be seen. I made
a cup of tea and got back into bed to sip it at my
leisure. I felt a weight on my eyelids and a sharp
pain in my head. Rays of sunlight flowed softly
between the thick shades. I drew back the
curtains. The warmth of the sun gave me the
strength to receive another day. I set the tea aside.
I couldn't taste what I was drinking anyway. I had
lost my sense of taste and I couldn't remember

whether I had added sugar to the tea. After a bit, I heard Camilia's laughter pealing like tiny bells as she climbed the stairs and approached the apartment door. She was carrying some things so I opened the door for her. One of the militiamen stood behind her: that same young man who had come by the other day and asked us to go down to the shelter. "I went to a nearby street to buy some food, thinking that from the calm over there might be good for me. We didn't have anything to eat," she added, laughing and pointing at the young man next to her. "He insisted on helping me. His name's Ranger. Just imagine—ha ha ha—Who has a name like that?" I greeted him cautiously. He remained silent, staring at me as a cold, neutral smile spread across his face. Camilia came inside and I shut the door behind her without inviting the young man in, and I followed her into the kitchen.

"Who is this guy?"

"He's a fighter from headquarters."

"I know, I know, I've seen him hanging around near the building a couple of times, but what's he doing here?"

"Oh Maha, why do you always have to make things so complicated, he's always saying hello and offering to help me."

"Listen to me, Camilia. Ever since I started living by myself, I haven't let anyone inside my house."

"But he's different, he's nice. And he promised to introduce me to the other guys so I can interview and film them."

I interrupted her angrily, "You can shoot your film someplace far away from here. The city is full of guys like them. Why'd you have to choose them?"

"I liked the way he looked," Camilia said flippantly, adding, "Besides, what do you expect me to do now that he's here?"

I wanted to tell her that he was a militiaman, that she shouldn't ever forget that, that he was different from Ghassan and Nadim. I wanted to tell her that he was cut from a different cloth. Instead, I found myself marveling at all the anger that had overcome me. The young woman standing before me smiled as though she had no connection to what had just happened or what was going on, as though no sparks of malice had ever pierced her heart. Had her detachment from the war over the years inoculated her against any real fear? In her simplicity, did she see him as nothing more than a helpful young man who said hello to her, as she described him to me just now? What neighborhood he came from, how he got started fighting: knowledge she set aside in order to make her work easier. Let's just wait and see where this knowledge leads us!

The rain that poured down all day didn't prevent me from visiting my hometown up in the mountains. I didn't have an umbrella but I did have a raincoat that Ghassan had left at my house once. It was a little too big for me. I rolled up the sleeves and cinched it around my waist with a belt made of the same material. I packed some essentials in my little suitcase. I always kept a bag handy in case I decided to go up to the mountains. To me, those visits always felt like going abroad, like traveling from one world to another. Even in the most violent of times, that place high above sea level experienced an entirely different conflict. Once I had packed my stuff, I left my apartment to set off with my neighbor Mansour, who worked as a driver, never taking even a single day off. Mansour didn't show up that day, though. He hadn't visited me for months. He must have been upset with me over the last time, when I refused to open the door for him. I told him that I was too busy to visit my father. He left without saying his stock phrase—"Good bye, do you need anything from home?"—and I hadn't seen him since. I had a car but I stopped driving it, leaving it parked behind the building instead. I used to drive it to pick up my paycheck at the end of every month. Every time I took the car out, I was stopped at the checkpoint in the middle of the street, the one located no more than three buildings from mine.

I told the guy with a huge weapon slung over his shoulders, who was leaning slightly in my direction, "I'm Maha Salman," and then reminded him, "I live in that brown building." I sensed his patience wearing thin, as though he had been forced to endure that same sentence hundreds of times each day. He repeated his request like an automaton: "ID and registration." I gave him my ID and the car registration and remained silent, never looking directly at him. He flipped through them one page at a time, then strolled around the car. He scrutinized my face for a few moments, as though he'd just caught me in an embarrassing situation and then asked me to pop the trunk. I opened the door slowly, got out of the car, and silently opened the trunk. The putrid smell of his sweat reeked. He searched thoroughly, fidgeting nervously, but didn't find anything of interest. I could see the anger in his eyes and emanating from his face like hot smoke. He retreated a little bit, stiffened, and handed my papers back to me. He stood there staring at me as I shut the trunk and returned to my car. I sat back down in the driver's seat and brushed the dust from my hands: an innocent student who had passed her test. I move on. *You son of a bitch.* Hadn't he stopped me once before, even calling me by name? *Hey, hey, you... Maha Salman, give me your ID and car registration!*

He wouldn't be stopping me again that day. I'd cross the street on foot. To be sure, walking has its disadvantages as well. At some point, I'll become a public spectacle for call and response, for the kind of conversation that an armed man shoots at an unarmed woman. Perhaps simply feigning deafness wouldn't be enough. It would be better to pretend to have lost all senses, to play dead. Isn't that what he wanted me to be anyway? But I regained my composure and figured that pretending to be dead would be worse than the alternatives. They wanted to transform the living into the waking dead. Otherwise, why would they spend all the hours of their nights and days on this street, under the very building where I lived?

When I passed through the building's iron gate, the morning air chilled me. I opened my mouth to swallow as much as I could. I felt like my nose could no longer provide me with enough oxygen, like I wanted to swallow all of the spring air with a single breath. It had rained all day and the asphalt was a glistening black, but I had never seen such powerful sunlight. Everything around me seemed radiant, silent, and bleak. The buildings that overlooked the end of the street stood as silent as long-abandoned ruin. Smells, garbage, and neglected things had collected there. Sunlight beamed down on these ruins and transformed them so that they resembled a Greek amphitheater. A feeling of boredom came over me as I saw the eyes of militiamen, who had begun swarming all around the building. Their stares didn't bother me anymore. The mask I used to hide my facial expressions whenever I saw them was a success that morning: eyes fixed straight ahead toward the distant horizon without expressing even apathy; mouth held neither in anger nor in a smile; ears straining to hear the first word out of them without looking like it; and the head actively working to suppress my loathing, to prevent me from exploding like a cluster bomb in that narrow space. *Stop! Where are you going? What's your name? Where do you live?* The questions I'd been expecting to hear, but I walked that morning and silence floated all around me. Once I had advanced several meters and left the vacant eyes behind me, a wave of unbridled laughter flooded over me. This was my only means of fighting back. I laughed and squeezed my palms together tightly. This was my own private method to help me cross the checkpoint, the checkpoint that took me to the end, the end that might become my end, an end I sought out defiantly, like a gambler with nothing left to lose.

My footsteps on the moist asphalt sped up as I moved away from my street. There, at the bend in the road, cats were fighting near a mountain of garbage that had been piling up for days. The number of cats in the streets had multiplied and so had their meowing. But it was the rabid dogs that

truly scared me. I asked the driver standing near
his car, "Taxi?" The driver stopped calling out for
passengers. He quickly got in his car and hopped
back into the driver's seat. I got into the back and
the car shot off toward the mountains. There were
taxis parked on the side of the road waiting to take
passengers to the South or to the Bekaa Valley. A
man called out for a fifth passenger so that he
could fill his car to the maximum before taking
off. The roofs of the metal shacks in the area
adjacent to the parking lots seemed vast and
endless: houses made in a hurry, as if their owners
had planned to live in them for only a limited
time. But that limited time had become an entire
lifetime. Under the hulking iron bridge, the filthy
roads teemed with cars crossing every which way,
carts carrying vegetables, clothes, and shoes
passing by one another. On the other side were
carts that had taken up permanent residence. The
sounds of explosions rang out. For a few moments
everyone listened closely to them. They were far
away. Life continued its cycle and people went
back to their work and their thoughts. But when
the sounds got closer, everyone started running in
all directions, and in a few minutes the street was
empty. It returned to its normal state: silent and
bleak. It became empty except for their smells, as
though the masterful fingers of a magician had
passed over their heads and hid them up his
sleeves.

The places looked different from one area to the next, but the people's faces looked the same wherever I went. The humiliation written in their eyes couldn't be mistaken. The faces looked alike everywhere I went. They resembled the faces of the people I saw in the shelter or on the street near my apartment when the women hurried to fetch water and bread, savoring these passing moments and staving off death. When the Farid al-Atrash song "You and Me and Nobody Else" started playing, the driver rocked his head in time with the lyrics and sometimes even anticipated them. The he looked at me in the rearview mirror. He let out a staccato whistle and a long *ahhhh*. "May God have mercy on your days, Farid," he muttered. The car zoomed off with us toward the mountains. How animated life seemed from behind the glass of the car window, free of even a trace of death's grime.

It would take an hour and a half to reach my hometown up in the mountains. I'd see my father lying in his bed and the cat would be curled up comfortably in front of the door. My lungs would expand to breathe in the scent of the large jasmine tree, which scratched its aging branches into deep indelible grooves all along the house's stone walls. I'd see its wet green leaves glistening in the sunlight. I'd ask my father about his health and he'd tell me about the pain in his joints, about the frailty of his body and his loneliness. I'd read my sister's letters and reread them aloud to my father, who could no longer read because of his weak vision. Umm Mansour would come as soon as she heard I had arrived and her voice—high and shrill like a train whistle—would deafen me as she told me about the girls who had gotten married, girls who were much younger than me. I'd ask myself what I was doing there. I could have called Mansour and asked him to bring me the letters instead. I looked out at the sea through the car window. I could still see the sea from there. The views weren't blocked yet. I rolled down the window and stuck my entire head out of the car as though I wanted to move closer to the seawater, to touch it with my lips, my mouth, my eyelashes. Its waves turned whiter when they approached the shore. Then, no sooner had they spread forth than they receded again toward the deep. A powerful wave rose up and soaked the sandy shore all the way up to the edge of the pavement. The angry wind intensified. There was no way to avoid breathing in the putrid air that stunk from garbage and sewers, emanating from houses whose inhabitants were blessed with tranquility. The driver turned down the radio, looked in the small rearview mirror in front of him and asked me where I was from and what I did for a living.

How long had it been since I last visited my father, four months, five? Maybe more. I realized how much the place had changed since that last visit. The road that once led to our house in the middle of the *hara* was blocked off by a giant cement wall with stairs cut right into the center of it. In place of the road, a wide street had been carved out that bisected the town from one end to the other. The expanses of almond and olive fields had been converted into a wide road with stores built on both sides, which the town, with its dwindling number of inhabitants, didn't even need. Some of the almond trees could still be seen flowering behind the stores. It was spring and the scent of the almond flowers was absorbed into my pores, the fields were fragrant with the smells of wet earth. At the time, I wanted to duck quickly into the house. I wanted it to remain my house, I wanted to smell its ancient aromas, and I wanted the comfort it had always offered me. I slept in the sitting room that night. My brother's family had come in from Kuwait. My brother's wife was sleeping in my room. She suffered from asthma and the doctor had advised her to go back to Lebanon and convalesce. My mother's spirit no longer roamed the rooms of the house, and hadn't for a long time. My delicate mother died before the war could sneak up on her. She died without seeing the town burn, without seeing her neighbors in the Christian neighborhood leave their homes, their food still stored in jars.

My mother's neighbors left their homes a long time ago. I was in Beirut at the time. The weather was cold. We drank a lot of wine at lunch. There was no heat but we were young women, we could handle the cold. We finished drinking the wine. There was a knock at the door and I told Intisar, who lived with me and who was waging the revolutionary struggle with the measly income she received at the end of every month, "If it's one of your friends, take them into the living room because I'm not leaving this room." Mazen showed up with his red face and wide eyes. "Did you hear what happened?" Whatever happened didn't matter to us. We had drunk a lot and didn't expect anything worse to happen. "They killed Kamal Jumblatt!" He didn't say another word. I remember that I laughed. What an idiot! I laughed again and Intisar stared at me. "He's going to die for sure, he's going to die," I said in what sounded like a whisper. "Why not? It would have been stranger if they hadn't killed him." A few moments of silence passed. Mazen remained standing and looking at me. I told Intisar, "Go get another bottle of wine and bring Mazen a glass." When she came back out, I told Mazen, "Drink up. Make it easier for us to understand one another." Pouring him some wine, Intisar asked, "Is it true what you're saying, or are you just screwing with us? Tell me the truth." Before letting him respond, I let out a choked cry. I don't know how I was able to sleep. The next morning, Intisar brought the newspapers and I saw his picture everywhere. I saw the destruction approaching, inexorably sweeping everything in the town along with it. It was much worse than we anticipated. How naïve we were.

My mother passed away before the war could force her out. She was radiant and a dreamer. Now I ask myself how she managed to give birth to four children when she was so full of her own dreams. "Make us some bread, Hayat!" my father would tell her. My mother didn't know how to make bread. My grandmother made it instead. My father opposed this, protesting, "I want to eat from my wife's hand, even if it's only once." My mother didn't make bread, instead wetting it and sprinkling it all around for the birds that made nests in the cracks of the walls. My grandmother boarded up her *qabu* and went to live with my mother, her only daughter, when she got married. My grandmother raised us and lived in our house. My mother remained in my life like a phantom, always passing from one place to another. That's always how my mother appeared to me in my dreams. She passed near my bed and pulled the blanket up until it covered my shoulders. Her eyes were vacant, looking at my face without actually seeing me. I tried to touch her hand and speak to her, but she was always on the verge of leaving. The wind outside blew away her shawl and the brilliant white *mandeel* that had been tied around her head like a dazzling crown her whole life. My grandmother's personality—the men's sister, as my dad always called her—was the opposite of my mother's. She accompanied my father to funerals, drove the women to mourn for the deceased and wailed over his head, staying up all night with the family. At our house, my grandmother put the chicken in the coop in the evening, picked olives, and strung the onions up on a line. She cleaned and dried the almonds and the apricots. She bathed us, combed our hair, hurting us and making us cry. Throughout her short life, my mother's cheeks were always red; when we were young, her cheeks would always turn red from bashfulness. When my brother Bashir went to America, she kissed him and then went into her room to cry, embarrassed to cry in front of my father. She would take out his letters and read them over and over. "A letter from the land far away from the homeland," she used to say. She kept those letters and read them at night after my father had gone to sleep.

My mother didn't look like other mothers. Her scent wasn't like those of other mothers. It was more like those of the relatives who came to visit from distant places bearing gifts and sweets.

My grandmother took care of all the chores. Umm Mansour came over to help clean the house and prepare the food for storage in the fall. When Umm Mansour started to tell my grandmother stories about the women in town with bad reputations, my grandmother would raise her slender index finger to her mouth to shush Umm Mansour. But Umm Mansour wouldn't shut up, changing the subject to something she thought wouldn't upset my grandmother and wouldn't result in her being shushed again.

Our house changed after my grandmother's death. A silence settled over it like we had never experienced before. My mother didn't change. She remained as silent as ever. But her silence seemed more defined somehow as we started asking her about household affairs, questions we had previously directed toward our grandmother. She didn't know where my grandmother kept the tablecloths that we used for holidays or the special pans for making pastries and other treats. It was as if she were discovering things about her house for the first time. The burden of illness didn't help her discover things about her house but sapped her strength further and sped the decay of her already emaciated body. My mother didn't live long after my grandmother's death. She lasted just one year. She passed away before the war could get to her and before seeing what befell Umm Jiryis, the traveling fabric saleswoman who was found dead one day on the side of the road, the women's fabrics, still soft to the touch, flapping all around her under the hot sun. Umm Jiryis used to visit us every Thursday. The town women always came to see what new fabrics she had brought. She used to spend the night with us and leave early Friday morning for another town. The women didn't pay her in cash but in installments. Umm Jiryis entrusted her accounts notebook to my mother, left it with her. When my mother's illness worsened, Umm Jiryis began visiting her more regularly. She sat for long hours on the front doorstep. She stopped asking my mother to watch over the notebook. When the winter sun finally emerged after long bouts of rainfall, Umm Jiryis came to peel pomegranate rinds for my mother, which my grandmother then hung up on thin fibrous ropes from the attic ceiling. It got easier for my grandmother to reach the attic in her later years once my father built stairs for her that began right in front of the kitchen door. Umm Jiryis would put the pomegranate seeds in a deep bowl after peeling the fruit completely. My mother would take some seeds, put a few in her mouth, and then fall back into her prior reverie. Sometimes she said a few incoherent words that had absolutely no connection among them. She asked whether my younger brother had returned home yet. His was the only name still left in my mother's memory. She always repeated it, even during the coma she fell into a little while before she died. Umm Jiryis would talk to her but my mother wouldn't hear a thing until she gently patted her lap and squeezed her hand to bring my mother back and reconnect with her. My mother would take some grains from her hand and ask what time it was, pointing to the sun that had begun to slink down toward the horizon.

When my brother returned after seventeen years away, my mother had grown old and the illness was rushing her toward the end of her days. My brother was still young in my mother's weak memory and had never grown up. She covered her face with the *mandeel* when they told her that he was her son. She couldn't believe it. She didn't know him. She said hello to him icily and hid her hand under the *mandeel* covering her face and wrapped around her chest. He told her, "I'm your son," and embraced her. My mother's cheeks turned red like someone in love for the first time. When she spotted the large brown mole on his earlobe, she knew that he was her son. She pulled the scarf away from her mouth, kissed him and cried. Sometimes when she saw me sitting in my pajamas next to my brother, she

started biting her lips at me and moving her head
a little, that is, intimating to me that I should go
change my clothes somewhere else. Then she
would remember that he was my brother Bashir
and would start asking, with bitterness apparent
in the depths of her green eyes, what was wrong
with her, a sad, weak smile on her lips. My
brother stayed with us for three months and my
mother honored him like a dignified guest; he
thanked her like a guest, too. She wasn't worried
about him when he went out and came back late;
she fell asleep before he returned. She didn't do
that with my brother Saleh. Seventeen years were
enough for my mother to feel like she had lost
her son forever.

After a little while, I'll reach my hometown and
pass through the Christian *hara*, which had been
emptied of its people. Instead, townspeople who
had grown up during the war years now lived in
what remained of their houses; as did those who
had gotten married and had children. The
children were born there, and so the homes and
birthplaces of those departed Christians would
also remain in the children's earliest memories, in
their dreams. Everyone's memories got mixed up
in these houses and in other such places,
memories of those who had died and those who
had been born. As I passed through that

neighborhood, I pictured the crowds that had gathered that day, carrying everything they could with them. They packed everything into bags and suitcases. Every woman took pictures of her family with her and left the keys to her house with a neighbor. She picked up her youngest child and left. The women talked a lot as they left, saying what they could say and what was impossible to say. The men left silently, a silence that hurt worse than anything they could possibly have said. My father was among those who came to say goodbye to them. He couldn't bring himself to shake anyone's hand and say goodbye; he couldn't embrace any of his friends. He remained there, standing by the side of the road, watching them get into their cars and drive away. Their farewell was different from the subsequent farewell when the Palestinians left Beirut. A man approached my father as he left town and rebuked him, saying: "This is how we build our country?"

The living room was almost completely dark when I returned home after the Christians had all left town. It was 8 PM. My father was sinking into the cushy chair on the balcony. I looked at him through the translucent glass and walked over to him. The lights of the capital were shimmering like stars that had fallen into the sea. Without turning toward me, inclining his face down toward the city, he said, "The very thing I warned you about down there came up here." His eyes were shining with sorrow. "This is how we build our country? Did you hear what that guy said to me?"

I never once saw tears in my father's eyes. I used to be afraid of him when he was angry, so I would run and hide in places he didn't know of. My father got angry but never cried. Did madness descend upon us that day or did we go to it? Did madness force itself upon us or had we been clearing the way for it, encouraging it? Is that how we build our country? What could I do to stop those menacing sounds, which engulfed every certainty? That night, a man whose hair had turned white started to cry. Well, he didn't cry exactly; rather, his face spewed water. "Even mountains spew tears," Umm Mansour said later that evening. "This insane violence won't swallow us," she added. "Never." I wanted to believe her. The moment my father cried, a profound feeling of fear was carried away from me, a fear I'd had my entire life. I was overcome with a joy made ambiguous by a kind of motherly sadness, a joy I buried in my bosom like a disgrace.

From that day forward, my father started to grow old. Maybe he had started before that night, but I hadn't noticed. Everything in town seemed to age. During the last meeting with the guys that Ghassan attended, Nadim said that we couldn't guarantee protection for anyone and that the best thing our Christian comrades could do would be to leave town. Our comrades left that very morning. Many others left as well. They left the keys to their houses with us, and even though we eventually lost them, the new residents didn't need them anyway.

In those few months, I realized an elderly man could be as difficult to care for as a breast-feeding baby. My father had changed a lot, as though he had aged a few years all at once, an aging that nobody likes, that tugs at the body as it slides down toward its ending. In the past, I was constantly prepared to fight with him. Perpetual bickering. We had fought ever since I left home and moved to live by myself in the city. Whenever he came to visit, I would rush to hide all traces of Ghassan in the apartment: put the shaving kit in the medicine cabinet, throw his pajamas in the laundry basket and cover them with a dirty towel. I'd tell him I was living with a female teacher from Tripoli. That may have been true the first year; it was also true the second year while Intisar was living with me. But I kept on using the same lie during the years that followed. When I went up to my house in the mountains, I took a Valium with me, swallowed it and listened politely to whatever he had to say. There was no use trying to have a conversation with him because he talked without listening. He always told me I was a stubborn girl and that I didn't understand, that I was idealistic and worked with people who exploited me and didn't respect me. That was how he had always described my friends from work. Then I'd go to my room, pack up all my stuff, and carry my suitcase back the way I'd come, swearing I would never visit the house again.

When I went into the house, I saw him lying in his bed. They had moved it from the bedroom into the sitting room. Maybe he was afraid they would forget about him if he stayed in his room. He said that he felt alone and neglected there, that he never had any visitors. He would leave the front door open so Umm Mansour could come by every morning to make him lunch and to clean his bedroom and bathroom. She would only set foot in the other rooms when my brother Saleh and his family were visiting from Kuwait. He was lying in bed when I arrived. He raised his arms toward me and propped up his feeble frame to give me a hug. I leaned in toward him and gave him a kiss. His face was cold and his chin was rough, with sharp white whiskers. "Why don't you shave your chin?" I asked him. He answered that his hands shook uncontrollably and that he always cut his face. My brother Saleh had given him an electric razor as a gift, but there was never any electricity. He pulled the green box out from under his bed and opened it, showing it off to me. Then he closed it and put it back where it was, saying that he was waiting for Mansour to come and give him a shave. A new picture of my father was engraved in my memory: his unsoft face, and his dark wool clothes.

My sister Reem's letters were accompanied by pictures of her and her family. In front of their large house, her Greek-American husband stands behind a green lawnmower, his eyes visible beneath a wide-brimmed straw hat. Her younger son is in a bathing suit, lounging on an orange towel and looking at the little dog resting in front of him. She is behind him, down on her knees, looking at him. They are all smiling. Anyone who looks at them can tell that their future is unmistakably bright, that their skies will always remain cloudless. I stared at the overwhelmingly green pictures, wondering what the color green might look like in a city that had lost all its color. Does destruction have its own color? And what color is it? What were Beirut's colors in the summer of '82? One day I found myself in the very house behind my sister's husband in that picture. The green yard was just as it looked in the pictures, lined with roses and other colorful flowers. At the other end of the garden there was a small pool, its clear water reflecting the blue of the sky. When I first arrived there, my sister embraced me. I asked to see my letters, all those letters I wrote to her from back in '75 until that day. I had written letters over the course of seven years, and when I got there, I told her how I felt as though I'd lost my memory and that I needed to read my letters. That way, I might be able to get reacquainted with myself, to reconnect the years that had been amputated from my life like limbs off a body, to remake those places I had started to lose. "I see my life anew, like a puzzle I hold in my hands but am unable to solve. I have no idea where to even start." I read that in one of my letters. Then I said to her, in another letter, "Don't be concerned by the length of my letters. Writing to you is a whole lot cheaper than seeing a psychiatrist." I discovered that what I had written was actually quite intimate, and that I would never dare reveal so much to her now. I started to imagine her completely engrossed in reading my letters, and smiled at the idea of her sitting in the rocking chair with green cushions, her face full of questions. Many things happened to me when I visited my sister. I tried in vain to recall them. When I went to stay at her house in New York, I carried her little son and I asked her about his citizenship: "Will he be Lebanese like you or Greek like his father?" She answered me coolly, "Well, he'll be American, just plain American." I felt as if she wished me harm but I didn't know why I felt that way, exactly. When she asked me if I wanted a glass of brandy as an aperitif, I told her I'd prefer a glass of *araq*, although I'd never cared for the taste of *araq*. I didn't say a word throughout the entire evening, and when she rose to clear the plates from the table, I got up to help her but couldn't come up with a single thing to say. That summer, I spent my days fixated on televised images of the Israeli invasion. At night I waited moment by moment for dawn to come so I could call Lebanon. "The calling rates are much cheaper then," she always said. Reem's pragmatism infuriated me, and so did that mind of hers, so organized and clear: regimented in speech, behavior, and laughter. How my sister had changed and how life had created a distance between us. One Sunday she tried to cheer me up by inviting some of her American girlfriends over for a garden party. One of them started talking to me as though she had known me for a long time: "You know, I feel really bad for your family in Lebanon, but why in the world did you let foreigners live in your country and then, on top of it all, let them have guns? They're nothing but terrorists, you know, and fighter jets can't tell the difference between you and them." "Oh yes. It's quite tragic," interjected another. In time, my sister started behaving differently toward me. She began treating me like a head case, like someone she had to take care of who was going through a crisis. She called me from her office several times a day, asking, "What are you up to?" I found myself having to make up little white lies. I found that "Just reading" was the most effective and easiest lie. I wasn't actually reading, of course, but sometimes walking around the house and other times lying down on the couch with my eyes closed in front of the television, which went on yapping and droning nonstop.

Reem's husband kissed me on the cheek when he came home and asked how my day was, what I had done. Then he told me about the opening of some new mega-mall that I had to go and see during the day. I nodded, pasting a neutral smile across my face. I knew that he couldn't do anything to help me and had no better way of communicating with me than this exaggerated, feigned interest. He also knew that I hadn't done anything all day because he came home and found me still in my pajamas; I hadn't washed my face or brushed my hair yet. The relationship that evolved between us was simple. He would play the role of gracious host and I would play the part of the guest who left a light footprint. But his lies didn't annoy me, and his game didn't bother me either. It actually comforted me and didn't require any conversation on my part if I preferred simply to remain silent. I was always silent while my sister Reem was talking. I never heard what she was saying, but I could tell that her voice was clear and heartfelt. I stared at her, tracking her pupils and the movement of her lips. Maybe she didn't hear what I said either, but simply expressed disapproval and bewilderment at the way I lived my life. I don't know how Reem ever got used to that country or accepted all of life's contradictions. During her first few years there, it was hard for her to get citizenship, even after she got married. That was because of some information about her "terrorist" past, as they put it. Nearly losing her patience, she told me, "Yeah, yeah I remember how I was part of a group of people who did sit-ins at the university. I was just a kid back then." I can still remember when she said goodbye to me when I was returning to Beirut. "Come back, save yourself and build a life for yourself here in America." I kissed her, choking back a powerful urge to cry out loud, as though I was losing her forever. I never saw her again after that. I'm not even certain anymore that memories are what bring people together, but that it's the act of living, its spaces and its smells, its moments of joy and sorrow.

"Read the letters aloud," my father said. I gave him the pictures and he put on his glasses and then looked at me. I reread the letters. How did my sister remember all those names, where did she get them all? There wasn't a soul in the family or the neighborhood whose name she didn't mention. In our last phone conversation, I told her that Marwan had blown himself up with a bomb strapped around his waist. But then she asked about him later and sent him her warmest greetings. Why am I remembering all of these things now? Suddenly, I remembered the time Ghassan wrapped his arms around me when we met at the airport. *Is it true, Ghassan, that people greeted them with roses and basil? Don't look at me like that, I can hear you saying that it's a lie, a media hoax as I was following the news of the invasion and the siege, and I can't believe it. Just let me ask about everything and don't interrupt me.* But in that moment I didn't ask anything else. I was jealous of him, a jealousy beyond words; jealous of his eyes, his fingers, his head and heart; jealous of his presence in Beirut during the summer of '82. I cried. When I told him how I had dreamed of losing my memory and that memory had became a stomachache I always had, he smiled and told me that the war was over. Together, we all believed that it was over. But we were moving ever closer to the final devastation, which turned into a chronic condition we slept in and woke up to. When he left me to go up to the mountains, Ghassan shrugged and asked, "What can I do if the world around me has gone mad?" He didn't do anything and I didn't do anything. I let him go in silence to the destiny that awaited him.

At Ghassan's funeral, I sat at the end of the room, across from all the women wailing around his coffin. I sat like someone out of place, leaning my head forward. The women whispered to each other between one elegy and the next. "It's her, her, her," one of them said. "She's old enough to be his mother," said another, motioning toward me from the corner of her eye. I couldn't see his face. Some women stood up, turned and forcefully thumped the sides of the coffin with bouquets of flowers they held as they circum-ambulated the bier. Flower petals scattered and fell all around them like leaves falling from a tree on a blustery day. *I love you so much I'd die for you*, he had said to me, but that's not why he died. The lamentations grew louder the moment that the *zaim* entered the room filled with the women dressed in black. The women's voices grew louder. The male presence heightened the intensity of their crying. Ghassan's mother beat her chest even as her eyes never left the coffin. She didn't look at the *zaim*; she didn't look at anyone. One of the women held a picture of Ghassan and spun with it, dancing. Many of them let their white *mandeel*s slide off their heads, some put them on the ground, still others wrapped them around their shoulders. I wanted to be alone with him at that moment, and I fought back a passionate urge to reach out and touch his cold hand.

Bodies moved, bent, groaned, burned up, suffered. The sound of choked screams. Of loud screaming. Crying. Weeping. Then silence. *Mandeel*s fell from the women's hair, their shiny hair styled precisely. Some were brunettes. Some let a little gray adorn their once raven hair. His mother's body bent, my body bent, screamed, moaned, hurt. I placed my hand on my stomach. "My son," she said, "I weep for the child I never had." There wasn't a soul who didn't recognize the *zaim*'s face and voice. Everyone knew him. Their heads seemed long after the thin white *mandeel*s had fallen to their shoulders. Some tried to pull the *mandeel*s back up, but they refused to stay. After a while the women no longer cared whether their hair could be seen with the *mandeel*s no longer cinched around their necks. Their necks were exposed as the *mandeel*s slipped down their, sad and crooked, as though they too mourned. The women had become bound by sorrow, the common property of absence, they became the effects of death, of legend. Only the religious women maintained their grip on the *mandeel*s, kept them tight around their heads, their necks.

Ghassan remained absent, silent, cold. Had those moments been real or a dream? He had truly gone to his death. His dreams drove him out to that open space on a scorched hill for days and nights. There, death took on another meaning. That's how he died twice: once when he lost his life and once when he couldn't give his death the meaning he so desired. Maybe everyone dies like that. "I'm the martyr's mother," I heard his mother repeat in an absent and choked voice.

I went out for some fresh air and had trouble catching my breath. Pain seared into my wrists. I squeezed my hands but the pain was buried deep inside like the blade of a sharp knife. I hurried toward the stairs. I couldn't pull myself together. I fell, grabbed hold of the handrail. Then I started to crawl on my belly until I reached the garden outside, where a large blue tent had been erected. Underneath it men were seated on chairs lined up into rows. I tried to cross the garden toward the street when I heard someone eulogizing the martyr, addressing the crowd, "My fellow Druze!" I couldn't stand up, it was if I were paralyzed. I buried my head in my hands and fell into a dark abyss.

Every day the sun rises only to show that there is nothing new under it. I would wake up, wash my face, and sit down to wait for evening to arrive. I wasn't certain at any point of the inevitability of evening. What if the sun simply stayed up forever? What if the order of the universe was altered and the earth changed the trajectory of its revolution? What if we were sucked into a black hole? Or fell into what was going on outside, the meaninglessness of our lives and the absurdity of our existence in this accursed world? What gave me the strength to persevere was my conviction that Ghassan was still with me. Sometimes I felt his presence inside me. I shivered and my body trembled. Light shone in my eyes as though my body were touching his. When I was with him, I felt as though I had the world in my hands and I could recover the all-encompassing warmth I had lost the moment my mother gave birth to me.

My brother Saleh came back from Kuwait. His wife was suffering from asthma. She has a nasty cough and was unable to sleep. She took to sleeping in my room, which remained sunny throughout most of the day. Sometimes I slept in my father's room and other times I slept in the sitting room adjacent to mine. My father snored. He snored during the few hours in which he actually managed to get some sleep. He left a candle burning on the ground near the door to guide his way to the bathroom at night. He got up to go to the bathroom several times each night, and every time the door opened, I could hear his shrill wheezing. My father came back to bed lethargically, dragging his feet. He groaned. When I asked him about his night, he said that nothing had happened and that I must have dreamed the whole thing. In the morning, he went out in front of the house wrapped in a brown *abaya* that my brother brought him from the Gulf. He didn't set foot outside until late morning, until after the sun had begun to beam down on the front yard. He would sit down in a chair, stretch his legs out on a low table in front of him and sleep for a while. After the sun moved to another position, his limbs got cold and stiff, so he would open his eyes and follow its rays. He would chase the sun, talking about it, about the pain in his legs. I had to spend long days in that house, until my brother's wife's health improved. I started preparing meals and setting the table. After my brother's wife had a coughing fit, it would take her a while to return to normal, and her lips might turn blue. When the veins in her neck started to bulge and the whites of her eyes expanded, I would take her frightened little girl out onto the balcony as my brother helped his wife inhale her special medicine.

Man ends up alone, my father said in a barely audible voice, as though he were continuing a conversation he had started long ago. He also said that he was still afraid of death, afraid of God actually existing because he hadn't believed in him his whole life and he was afraid of being punished. When he talked, he just moved his mouth. He stopped gesticulating, leaving his hands frozen under the blanket, as though he wasn't capable of lifting them to accompany his flowing conversation as he once could. I asked myself whether man ends up alone, whether he is always like that and just doesn't discover his solitude until he gets older. I started to distract my father from his solitude, reminding him of stories that he used to tell me in the past. I'd lie by telling him that I had forgotten the details, that I wanted to hear them again. Just then, he would adjust how he was sitting as a brilliant smile flashed in his eyes and he raised his voice to make it as clear and as strong as it had ever been. He embellished on the story that he had told me many times before with a new flavor or a new meaning, and sometimes he recited some aphorism that reflected his mood on that day.

During my last visit to see him, he didn't ask me why I stayed in Beirut—"The seat of corruption," as he used to call it. It was as though he had finally accepted his daughter, after years of refusing to do so. Or maybe he had let go of his last remaining desire to try to change her. It seemed to me that this acceptance might have come over us both. I, too, stopped resisting him or getting angry when he commented on something I said or something I did. I began accepting his refusal of my lifestyle without letting it upset me. I concluded that the remaining years of his life weren't enough for me to change him. Maybe I also lost the desire to change him or to change any other living creature. When I got up to put him to bed, he asked me why my face was so sallow, whether I had been sleeping well. To me, he seemed resigned to his weakness, as though he was getting ready for his final journey.

I no longer had any friends in town. My friends had all died or moved away. Whoever hadn't emigrated had settled in the city. Many faces passed by me in the town square but I didn't see any of my old friends. Strangers had begun moving into town ever since the first years of the war. Their families grew up. Some of them got married and went off to live by themselves.

Umm Mansour came by in the morning bearing vegetables and fruit that she had just bought. "Oof, can you believe how expensive everything is! We used to buy enough for the entire year for just 100 lira. Now look!" She showed me the two black plastic bags she was holding. "100 lira for just these few things!" She added, "Can you believe it?" Small cars from distant towns had to bring vegetables and fruit to our town ever since those who stayed behind stopped tending their farmlands.

My heart would beat faster the closer I got to my street in the city. I passed through many checkpoints, but the most dangerous one of all was the checkpoint near my building, which I suspected they set up especially for me. One minute, two minutes, then a third before I was able to enter the building and escape their stares, which burrowed into my back like barbs. When I opened my apartment door, I was bowled over by Camilia's smells, which clung to my things, to the whole place. In the bedroom, the bed was unmade and the soaking-wet bath towel was thrown on the ground beside it. Her nightgown was tossed casually, inside out, on the chair. Her smell overpowered my senses. I expected her to appear at any moment: from under the sheets, from behind the curtains, from inside the closet. But the house was as silent as it had been before she came to live with me. In the small living room, a neglected chair was left facing the glass door that opened onto the balcony, the very same chair I had moved ever since the street that the balcony looked out on to had become unsafe. The ashtray was overflowing with cigarette butts of various brands. The cushions were on the ground, arranged in a circle. Empty beer bottles were left beside them. Beautiful chaos soaked in the smells of living. I saw my house in a wholly different light. I went back to the bedroom and just stood there fiddling with the woman's things that had been strewn across the bedside table. I opened every box and closely examined every color, lifted the lid of the perfume bottle and sprayed it behind my ears and on the palms of my hands. It was as though, in that moment, I was hearing her breath nearby, as though I had just touched her in the mirror hanging in front of me, as though I had seen her ghost pass from the bedroom to the bathroom and then return to wrap itself in the thin sheet spread on the big bed.

Night was falling when I was awoken by a slight commotion in the house. Camilia was standing beside a bunch of household supplies. Ranger and a few other young men, some who worked with her on the film, were standing beside her. I don't know why the thought occurred to me that the war in the streets had just moved into my house. Outside were noises, closed roads, death; in here, on one of these mornings, we might find ourselves besieged in our own bedrooms: similar situations. What's the difference as long as we live through what's going on all around us as though it isn't really any of our concern?

Ranger started coming by every day. He ensured that we had electricity. Our apartment was the only one in the neighborhood where the electricity didn't get cut off. The television began blaring every night once again. Camilia and Ranger stayed up late watching TV with their friends: fighters and filmmakers. Our late nights weren't silent any more. Ghassan's ghost was absent; it disappeared as soon as Ranger showed up. It was impossible for the two of them to live in the same memory, as though my memory was partitioned to live two separate lives, two different desires. Why couldn't Ghassan and Ranger inhabit the same memory? What was this partition and how had it come about? How can memory be so fragmentary? It's like a road unfolding before us that we suddenly realize doesn't lead anywhere. Why was I so eager to see Ranger, even though, somewhere in my mind, I was afraid of him and his stares, which made me quiver? Every night I longed to see him. He had become a persistent need. I was amazed at how I received him when I actually did see him, as though I was trying to delay a joke that I was sure he would tell as soon as he arrived. He sat down on the couch and stretched his long legs out on the table, which was covered with a fabric ornamented with silk threads my grandmother had given me. But I was indifferent. Camilia looked into my eyes as though she realized what had come over me the moment he arrived. Her staring started bothering me, so I got up under the pretense that I had something urgent to take care of. I went into the kitchen and immediately came back out again to float around the house before returning to sit down across from them. That night Ranger came into the kitchen to cut carrots and cucumbers. I was standing near him. His smell was powerful. It seeped inside me. At that time, I thought of telling him how, at first, he used to scare me. I secretly asked myself if he had ever actually stopped scaring me. He took off his khaki shirt and had nothing left on but a white

undershirt. He was close to me and I saw the
hairs glistening on his chest. I forgot what I had
been doing in the kitchen as I listened to his
regular breathing and the occasional whistling
noise. Sometimes he would look at me and then
turn his head away, indicating that he was busy
doing something else. I wanted to drop everything and draw closer to him. A powerful desire
came over me: to run my hands over his body just
to prove to myself that we were alike somehow,
that his thoughts might resemble my own; to
touch him; to talk about exhaustion, exhaustion
from the difference that cannot be reconciled by
the union of two bodies, the difference that can
convert life into death and love into violence.

Ranger taught us how to play cards; I was
never very good. We started sitting around the
square card table for hours on end. Whenever
our group grew to more than four people, the
loser would sit out so that someone else could
rotate in. Ranger's friends and Camilia's friends
played and didn't leave until the early hours of
morning. But he stayed. I started sometimes
seeing people in the apartment whose names I
didn't know; they knocked on the door and came
right in, talking to Ranger as he sat and played
cards; sometimes they stayed the night. They
opened the glass balcony door and went out onto
the balcony, smoking and drinking beer and then
betting on who could throw the empty bottles

the farthest. The bottle would fly across the width of the street, sometimes smashing into the wall of the opposite building and shattering on either the adjoining balcony or the pavement. Sometimes it fell to the ground of the neighboring garden without breaking. Someone would look out from the opposite balcony, but he went back inside quickly after they spotted him. Our voices in the night and Camilia's laughing drowned out the sounds of violence that occasionally approached the building. The tape recorder blasted shrieking jazz. When Camilia heard something she liked, she would put her glass aside and rest her hand on the edge of the couch, trying to stand up and dance, barefoot, wherever she was. The friends took off, but Ranger stayed the night. With him sprawled out on the couch and us sitting on the colorful rug spread out on the ground, it seemed to me that whatever was in store for us would be even more dangerous and more harmful than whatever was going on outside. This wasn't an uplifting thought, so I quickly pushed it back in my head, watching his intent pleasure as he played with Camilia's hair, like someone petting a cat, someone who believed he was its sole master.

My relationship with Ranger swung back and forth, ebbed and flowed like the crashing of the tide. I rested my head on my pillow after locking the door securely behind me, listening to the explosions rumbling. I asked myself how long I would go on counting out the number of bullets fired and monitoring the moans of Camilia and Ranger. At that moment I yearned to see his bare chest, which was always concealed beneath a thin undershirt. When he brought one of his joints, he'd light it and hand it to me. I passed it directly to Camilia, who was sitting next to me. "Why don't you take a puff?" he asked me. I said I didn't care for the stuff. "Oof, you're so strict, you only do what you like," he grumbled, showing his sarcastic smile and extending his hand with another joint. Camilia took a deep puff, closed her eyes and said with plain distaste, "Leave her alone, just leave her alone," before smirking at me ironically. I grabbed the joint violently from him. The glasses of wine kept getting filled and emptied. It was night and suddenly I felt heavy drowsiness overwhelm me. I fell asleep right where I was.

I woke up at dawn, feeling a weight in my head. I couldn't get up from where I was, not even to sit. By the light creeping in from outside, I saw Ranger sleeping near me: his lifeless arm weighed heavily on my bare stomach. Camilia slept on the other side. I didn't say anything to Camilia the next morning. We didn't talk at all about the night before. I didn't intend not to talk, but I was overcome by the feeling that all talk was pointless.

When Nadim visited after he had returned from traveling, Ranger was there. They immediately started taunting one another as though they were born enemies. When Nadim got up in a hurry to leave, the expression on his face saddened me. He never visited us again and Camilia never called him anyway. During the last round of violence, Ranger never left our side. He became master of the house, without rival. He decided what we ate and when we went out. It became impossible to evict him from my life or Camilia's. Rather, he became the point of connection between us, as though his presence was the only excuse for Camilia to stay in my home. I started noticing how our relationship had come to have something like a daily rhythm, a routine that moved us from one day to the next and which we didn't know how to stop. He taught us how to play cards. He taught us how to bet and we came to know what awaited the loser. Ranger never lost, and we went on playing like the losers he wanted us to be, with indifference as our guide, with cigarettes and wine.

We didn't go out very often. When the situation got too violent, we moved down to Warda's apartment on the first floor. The shelter became a desolate place for us. Warda was still in

Cyprus waiting for her American visa. We stopped receiving word from her. I hadn't heard anything from her for three months. Rashad's sister Najla no longer came by the building. She took over her ex-husband Abu Ali's apartment after he left in the summer of '82. She followed him to Tunis and pleaded for him to put her back under his custody so that she could keep the apartment and live there. When I bumped into her by chance, she insisted that Warda was crazy, that she was frittering away the money that Rashad had left her in Cyprus. Then she said, with even more sarcasm, "Does she expect him to take her to America? What would she do there anyway?"

Ranger was master of the house, the absolute master. When Camilia wanted to go out one night to visit Muhammad, Ranger prohibited her from going. She headed toward the door, ignoring him, but he grabbed her hand, yanked her back inside and slammed the door violently, telling her, "Stay here, the streets aren't safe." But we didn't hear any noise outside. Camilia didn't believe him, and when she insisted on going out, he shoved her toward the couch, shouting in her face, "You're staying right here!" I didn't hear a peep out of Camilia for the rest of the night. When there was a knock at the door, she got up to answer it. It was Muhammad. His face looked yellow. "I was worried about you. This is the first time you've ever not shown up for one of our meetings." He had walked all the way over, and when he entered the living room, Ranger glanced at him but didn't budge: his body remained sunk into the couch, his long legs stretched out in front of him. He didn't like the way the doctor looked, the doctor whom Camilia embraced and took into the kitchen with her, where she was making dinner.

Camilia didn't eat anything that night. When Ranger curtly ordered her to eat something, she said she didn't care for canned fish. Ranger violently pushed his flattened palm against the back of her head and forced her down toward the plate in front of her, yelling, "You're going to eat this!" She tried to wriggle away from him. He pressed harder and rubbed her face in the plate of tuna.

"Leave her alone, she doesn't feel like eating!" Muhammad interjected.

"This is none of your fucking business! Who the hell are you to tell me what to do?"

Muhammad stood up and approached the two of them, raising his voice further, "I said, leave her alone!" At that moment, Camilia started sobbing loudly, covered her face with her hands and tried to escape. She headed for the bathroom. I found myself caught between the two of them, between Muhammad and Ranger. I grabbed the doctor's hand. I stood facing him.

"Please, shut up, shut up and don't say another word!" I told him in what I hoped was a whisper.

I knew that silence was his only hope, that his survival depended on it. Ranger shoved him backwards.

"Get the hell out of here. And don't ever come back to this neighborhood again, you understand me. Get out of here now or else!"

Camilia hurried back, her face still dripping with soap and water, and politely asked Muhammad to leave. I did the same.

The apartment had filled up with a large group of young men, Ranger's men. Their eyes were fixed on Muhammad's face, as though they wanted to tear him to shreds with their claws. As the doctor spun around and started to walk back downstairs, toward the outside, I heard words leaking out from between Ranger's teeth, "We'll deal with you later, you son of a bitch—" Muhammad turned toward him slightly, without responding, and then continued descending the stairs. At that point, Ranger kicked my cat Noosa, who had been lying peacefully on the carpet, a powerful kick as his curses shot out in every direction. Noosa went flying and crashed into the living room wall, fell to the ground and then ran off in terror, screeching horribly.

Camilia changed after Muhammad was kidnapped and executed. She came over to my house one day and her eyes were as humiliated as they had once been radiant, full of life. She was no longer the woman I used to know. Her voice no longer chirped from room to room with her coming and going, her scent no longer lingered in the corners of the house. She didn't go out at all anymore, staying in bed for days on end. Most of the friends who had collaborated with her on the film had left. They wanted her to go with them. She chose to stay under the pretense that she hadn't finished all of her work and didn't want to pack up and go back in such a hurry. Sometimes I thought she was doing all right despite her nausea. Sometimes her silence scared me. For two weeks straight I didn't leave her side. Her scents around the house thinned out even though she hadn't left. Her presence also seemed to thin out. I would have forgotten about her existence entirely had I not gone into the bedroom and saw her there, bedridden. Ranger visited us from time to time. When he saw her lying in bed and noticed her dullish yellow face, he walked into the room and turned his head apathetically, looking at me, and said, "What's up, does your friend have the plague or something?"

Camilia never finished shooting the film. She claimed that the story was too long and that she would never be able to finish it. Maybe the story had overtaken her so that she could no longer tell it.

Josefa came to visit us that morning. My God, how the seventy-year-old woman had changed, how gaunt she had become. But her eyes still shimmered with a resolute power. Josefa arrived at our front door and Andrea, now living in Josefa's apartment, opened it for her, holding a half-drunk bottle of dark beer. "I'm Josefa, the owner of this apartment," she told her. "I'm here to collect some of my things." Andrea stepped aside for her to enter. "This place is yours, take whatever you like." Josefa gathered up some belongings from her home and came down to have coffee with me. She asked about Lilian and Warda and, when I told her that neither of them was in the building anymore, she stood up and said that she had to be on her way to the checkpoint if she was going to make it home early. She said goodbye to me hastily and left.

They say that the war is going to end soon. I hear a lot of people saying that. Was that why the violence was escalating all around us, like the mouth of a volcano spewing sparks and lava, only to calm and let it all ooze away?

Ranger came over that night. Camilia sat on the big couch and remained silent. The bombing was intense that night. How violent it was! The shouting in the streets grew louder. Military

vehicles turned on their lights. They called
Ranger from downstairs. Hordes of boys from the
street went up to the military vehicles, whose
engines were revving powerfully. Ranger went
down and then came back up, panting, "There's
been an order to evacuate. They've got plans to
attack us, to attack the neighborhood. It's going
to happen within the next 24 hours." The sounds
in the street and in the adjacent buildings grew
louder: families fled the buildings for safer parts,
their echoes drifting far away, the slow footfalls
of the elderly as they walked close to the walls in
order to leave room for those younger than them
to move quickly down the stairs.

"Are they saying that the war is going to end
soon?" repeated one of the women hurrying off,
carrying her son in her arms. "They always say
that but it never ends." Ranger went downstairs
again and when he came back, he said that the
war was going to end soon and that we had to go
someplace safer in the meanwhile. I didn't
understand this contradiction: attacks on the
neighborhood even though the war was about to
end. I didn't like what he said about how the war
was going to end, just like that, while we waited.
Camilia broke her extended silence, saying, "So
the war's going to end, just like that, without any
warning? How boring!" Camilia turned toward
me and gazed into my eyes. Her look was
different: sparkling with extreme harshness. Then

she added that she wanted to play cards and that she wasn't going anywhere. "Let's play cards," I said. Ranger made fun of us and burst out laughing. He got up to leave but Camilia held on to him, "You aren't going to leave us now, are you?" "It's all a lie, they're not going to attack the neighborhood," I said, and then added, "But let's go down to the shelter anyway. It's safer there." They called for Ranger several times. He went out to the balcony and downed what was left of the wine. "I'll follow you," he said and then came in. Camilia filled his glass several times. Military vehicle searchlights shone on the apartment walls. We went down to the empty shelter. This time families didn't come to our building, but went to the back street shelters because they were safer. Everyone said that they were safer and I repeated it. Their departure amazed me. Our silence and our loneliness also amazed me. The two of us started playing cards against him and this time we were playing for keeps, conspiring against him. Playing for keeps: card-playing, conspiracy, and a war on the verge of ending.

Everything in the building shook, as though we were having an earthquake: explosions rang out, came closer; warning sirens, fire-truck sirens; the smell of coldness, the smell of rotting, the smell of closed and cold, desolate places. Light came from one candle near the shelter door that Camilia had left open. The chairs we had sat on playing cards during the previous nights were right where we had left them. Ranger looked tired. "Uh-uh, you're not going to sleep yet," Camilia told him. "The night is still young and we want to play cards. You promised." He took a glass of wine from her and drained it. Camilia lit some more candles, sat down to shuffle the cards, dealt. She looked at me and I returned her conspiring look. Our feet touched under the table. We played, she whispered to me, we cheated. We won: Ranger lost. What's wrong with him losing today? Sweat dripped from his brow like steam rising from a pressure cooker. "My turn," Camilia said. "Come lie down on the bed." Ranger's eyes shone. He was afraid of what was going on outside. "But I have to go join up with the guys," he said slowly and lazily. "Don't worry, nothing's going to happen," I told him. "I'll give you some pajamas and you just act like you have nothing to do with any of them when the others come, like you're one of us. Hide when you hear something and be afraid. The others are your enemies, right?" "Don't be afraid," Camilia told him. "We never win when we play cards with you. Should we stop now that luck is on our side?" "The war's almost over. We never played before and now we like to play," I said. "Who wouldn't?" Camilia added wickedly.

The two of us were masters of the situation, queens without a kingdom, without crowns. The

place was ours in all its emptiness, in all the
horror that surrounded us, the recurring noises
that reminded us of the state we were in. Horror
surrounded us but still we were two queens. The
king's throne collapsed, the king we had loved
ardently until the bitter end, until the desire to
annihilate took over. We downed our glasses.
Camilia brought a laundry line and we cut it into
four pieces. We tied each of Ranger's limbs to a
corner of the metal bed. "You never told us about
how you used to kidnap people, how you used to
interrogate them, how you used to torture them,
how you used to kill them. Come on, tell us all
about it now and we'll play kidnapper and
kidnapped. I'll be the kidnapper and you'll be the
kidnapped. Heh, what do you say?" Camilia
proposed. "Akh… you really squeezed my feet
together!" Ranger said, "Loosen the rope a little.
Don't squeeze so tight!" She went right on
talking, without listening to him. He looked
shocked, he didn't want to play this game, but he
did want to know how it was going to end.
Camilia stood behind him and looked down from
above his head. "Now, tell me. Why did you kill
the doctor who works in the hospital? Why did
you kill Muhammad?" Ranger laughed. "What,
have you started playing already?" he asked her.
"Yes, and don't say anything more than what's
asked of you. You killed him, that much I know.
But why?" Ranger laughed again and looked at

me questioningly, in astonishment really, as though to say, what's gotten into her? Had Camilia gone mad? "Untie me and I'll tell you why." He twisted his head toward me, "What's gotten into your friend?" I didn't reply. I saw a new flash in Camilia's eyes, as though the game was getting ahead of her and she was just trying to regain control. The game moved to a new level, and it was impossible for us to go back.

I had never seen a man with his arms and legs tied up except in the movies. I suddenly felt very thirsty. My throat was dry, I craved water but was unable to pick up my feet and move toward the shelter door. "Untie me!" His voice started to rise but then he suddenly fell silent. Sweat poured out of him and the noises outside drowned out our voices. My cat Noosa scratched the shelter door from outside. She let out a choked, furious meow. Ranger started yanking his hands up, trying to wriggle out of the bonds and to free his feet. The bed lurched beneath him, making a creaking sound that took our breath away. I was standing right in front of him, near his feet, which were still bound. I looked him square in the face and he asked us to untie him. He didn't dare scream because there were people outside who would have been very happy to learn of his presence. When he started to tell the story of how he kidnapped the doctor, I no longer saw him in front of me. I no longer blinked and my eyelashes stopped fluttering. I wanted to close my eyes but I couldn't, as though an invisible power had frozen them into two glass spheres. All things come to an end, I thought. Even violence reaches a point from which it cannot advance further. It will go on piling up on the violence that came before it, stacking up time and emptiness. It becomes like bare, unembellished lust. "I didn't mean to kill him. I just wanted to make him suffer, to scare him a little bit. I told him to confess when we blindfolded him and put him in the underground parking garage. He started asking me what he should confess for. I hit him. All the guys with me hit him. Then I told him to confess or else I'd cut his fingers off. I took his hand and placed it on the edge of an ashtray, making him think that we were really getting ready to cut off his fingers. But he laughed. When he laughed, all the blood rushed to my head. He was laughing at us, I thought, so I whacked him on the head with the butt of a rifle. I was angry at him for laughing. He was unconscious. I waited for him to come to, I shook him, I threw cold water on his face, but he was dead."

I tried to feel my hand. I tried interlocking my fingers but my hands were solid wood. Camilia's sobbing was louder than the noises outside. Then it faded into muted crying. The curses I heard were either hers or mine. I can see myself hitting him. I can see her beating him.

Take that for the years that we weren't allowed to enjoy. For the emptiness we suffered through. For our illusions. For all our fear. For our humiliation. Ranger's gun was lying near the card table. Just as I remembered that it was there, I saw it shining in Camilia's hand. Until then, we'd just been playing around, and our game was bearable, but it quickly got away from us and it was hard for us to regain control. Bang! One time. He screams. Bang: another one.

Are you the one crying or is it me? Is that coming from you or from me? Why is he silent? There is a silence in which we both feel an overwhelming solitude. Just his eyes were open, looking at Camilia. Is that you sobbing or is it me? Is that your face wet with all the water of the earth or is it mine? Are those our faces recovering their time, like creatures imagining they are reclaiming something stolen from them?

The building shook. We ran out of the shelter. Lights shone from the end of the street. They were coming. We ran back inside the shelter. Camilia continued her loud sobbing. "Shut up." I froze. I thought quickly. "Untie his cords! Come closer!" Her body quaked. My body quaked. She untied his hands. I untied his feet. "Help me lift him, come on! We're not going to leave him here." She lifted him from under his arms. His body was still warm. He was so heavy. I lifted him with her. We lowered his feet to the ground. We dragged his body, stumbling backwards. His body slipped from between our cold, stiff hands. We lifted him again and climbed the six stairs from the shelter to the building entrance, one step at a time. It was easier to drag him here. We opened the outer gate and dragged him outside the building, far from the gate. We took him farther than we would have liked, too far for us to see later, too far for memory to recover him. We left him there. Lights were approaching, gunshots and shouting. Camilia hurried inside the building. I heard her teeth chattering. "I'm cold," she said. She leaned on me. I nearly collapsed, but gained control of myself and held onto her arm. We climbed the stairs to the first floor. The world blazed like a fireball, orange melting into blue: blue that seemed briefly like the color when night turns to day, when the sky is serene and cloudless. Between the blue of death and the blue of a sky in which all meanings are lost, in which truth is mixed up with illusion; between the blue of death and the blue of sky there is a loss from which there is no return, which waits for me to master it. Then a noise disrupted the moment, snapped us out of our fear and pushed us toward an even greater one. A shell landed in front of the building, out where Ranger was. Camilia's body rammed into the banister. Dirt and asphalt pebbles flew in all directions. The sound of broken glass reverberated in my head. I fell and she collapsed on top of me. A bloody gash in my forehead. Pain in my lower leg. She felt her stomach with her hands. The pain! She stood up, dazed. I was still on the ground, too tired to stand.

The war is over. That's what they say. That's what the news broadcasts report and what the papers print. That's what the people, the children, and the carts on the street say. Camilia decided to return to England after learning that there was a child growing inside her.

"I'll go back and try to settle down," she said as she embraced me. "My child will become my homeland. He'll live through me and I'll live through him," she said, rubbing her stomach. "It'll be a beautiful child. It will have no father." She smiled as she said goodbye. I smiled, too. She said it was the first time she had ever seen me smile, adding that we all just might need some divine intervention to cure what ails us. I nodded and watched her make her way to the door, walk down the stairs, and leave.

The sun shone down on the backyard where the tanks had left deep craters in the earth. A gust of air whipped at my face. People passed on the street, walking lethargically, as though they had just woken from a deep sleep. The emptiness consumed me. I tried to focus on a single idea but it flew away from me like a bird. My hollowness hurt me. I couldn't feel anything. The war had taken everything with it when it finally departed, like people who carry all their possessions on their backs when they leave their homes, who take their pictures down off filthy walls—they take down their pictures, but the traces left behind are eternal reminders of their absence. Absence inhabited us. The sun rose higher in the sky but I was freezing. The best thing I could have done was go back in my room and shut the balcony door behind me.

I don't feel like going out, I don't feel like working. Today I have some time to think about what I want to do, tomorrow I'll think about it some more. They may say the war has ended but I haven't finished my story yet.

Notes

30: *inshallah*: "God willing."

36: *bayt*: In Arabic, *bayt* conveys both the sense of a physical structure that one lives in and also the more abstract sense of belonging to a place that feels like home.

77: Daraj Ja'ara staircase: A staircase that gives its name to the Darj Ja'ara neighborhood in Ashrafieh, a Christian section of Beirut.

96: *mandeel*: head scarf worn by Druze women.
majlis: literally, the place of sitting. Here, a Druze prayer room.

106: talisman: A piece of leather or tissue rolled and sewn, usually to take the shape of triangular pocket, containing a piece of paper on which a sheikh has written sacred religious words.

109: *qabu*: Typical of old Lebanese houses, this is a room with four (or more) arcades that begin as columns in the room's corners and arch to meet in the center of the ceiling.

111: *kitab al-hikma*: literally, "book of wisdom"; the Druze holy book.

136: *hurma*: literally, "woman." The substitution of this term for the traditional "Ms." or "Madame" signified a degradation in women's status.

181: *hara*: A large house comprised of smaller connected houses.

182: Kamal Jumblatt: Born in the Chouf Mountains of Lebanon in 1917, Jumblatt was the scion of a notable Druze family who went on to become an important force in Lebanese politics and national life. In 1949, he founded the Progressive Socialist Party (PSP) that called for the de-sectarianization of Lebanese politics, although its leadership has primarily been drawn from the Druze community. He later played a key role in the foundation of the Lebanese National Movement. Jumblatt was assassinated on March 16, 1977.

199: *zaim*: literally, leader. In the Lebanese context, a *zaim* is a political boss, but can also convey a sense of being the notable leader or figurehead of a particular neighborhood, community, movement, sect, or party.